"Uh Uh, Sweetheart. I Don't Intend To Make It Easy For You Anymore."

His voice was husky with suppressed passion when he spoke. "I'll be over at my cottage, waiting for you."

He settled back into the seat of his black Ferrari. That was clearly all he intended to say. More confused than ever, Jane swung open the door and climbed out. She didn't know which one of the conflicting messages on James's face and in his voice to heed: *Please come. Don't come.*

"I'll be there after supper, James," she announced firmly, and slammed the door.

CAROLE HALSTON

is the wife of a sea captain and she writes while her husband is out at sea. Her characters often share her own love of nature and enjoyment of active outdoor sports. Ms. Halston is an avid tennis player and a dedicated sailor.

Dear Reader:

Romance readers have been enthusiastic about Silhouette Special Editions for years. And that's not by accident: Special Editions were the first of their kind and continue to feature realistic stories with heightened romantic tension.

The longer stories, sophisticated style, greater sensual detail and variety that made Special Editions popular are the same elements that will make you want to read book after book.

We hope that you enjoy this Special Edition today, and will enjoy many more.

The Editors at Silhouette Books

CAROLE HALSTON
The Black Knight

Silhouette Special Edition
Published by Silhouette Books New York
America's Publisher of Contemporary Romance

SILHOUETTE BOOKS
300 E. 42nd St., New York, N.Y. 10017

Copyright © 1985 by Carole Halston

Distributed by Pocket Books

ISBN: 0-373-09223-7

First Silhouette Books printing March, 1985

10 9 8 7 6 5 4 3 2 1

Map by Ray Lundgren

America's Publisher of Contemporary Romance

Printed in the U.S.A.

Books by Carole Halston

Silhouette Romance

Stand-In Bride #62
Love Legacy #83
Undercover Girl #152
Sunset in Paradise #208

Silhouette Special Edition

Keys to Daniel's House #8
Collision Course #41
The Marriage Bonus #86
Summer Course in Love #115
A Hard Bargain #139
Something Lost, Something Gained #163
A Common Heritage #211
The Black Knight #223

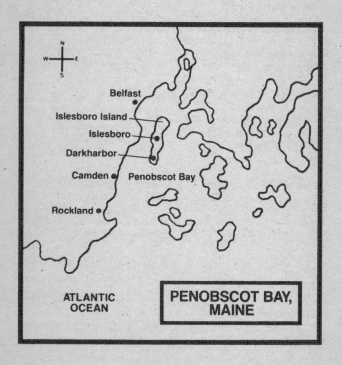

ATLANTIC
OCEAN

PENOBSCOT BAY,
MAINE

Chapter One

"These are *exquisite!* Absolutely *exquisite!* Helen, would you come over here and look at this?"

Jane felt her face growing warm with pleasure as well as with embarrassment at the fuss the woman was making over her display of needlework. Not that she wasn't used to having the people who came into the crafts co-op admire her work, but usually not with such volume and force. Everyone in the large room had stopped and looked her way.

"Where do you get your patterns? These aren't kits, are they?" the woman was demanding. Broad-shouldered and big-chested, with no indentation at the waist, her figure tapered to narrow hips and then incongruously elegant legs and dainty feet, shod in expensive kid pumps. She and "Helen," two wealthy matrons out for a day of "antiquing" and browsing for finds in quaint gift shops, had pulled up outside in a late-model Mercedes. Jane knew the type well, understood perfectly the regal, demanding manner. Lottie had been like that—though certainly more refined—before she lost most of her fortune.

"I make up my own designs," Jane replied courteously, feeling no need to explain that not only did kits bore her, they were also too expensive. As the two women admiringly examined each item, Jane was able to glean from the comments they exchanged that their decision was not *whether* to buy but *what* and even *how many*. While Jane didn't consider herself an artist, with every sale she invariably experienced the same sharp conflict an artist must feel when a painting or a sculpture he or she has spent many hours creating is about to fall into the possession of someone else, a stranger.

She loved each piece she designed and embroidered. If circumstances had been different, if she hadn't needed the money so badly, she would by far have preferred to give her work away rather than to sell it. Silly as her feelings were, she always worried whether each of her highly individualized creations would be getting a good "home."

Of course, she had never spoken any of these feelings aloud. To soothe Lottie's pride, Jane pretended that her needlework was just a pastime, not her salvation, and that her participation in the crafts co-op was more of a social outlet than anything else. True, she did look forward to those days, like today, when she tended shop and could chat with the other members present, primarily summer residents, and with the customers who dropped by, some of whom were tourists who had taken the ferry over to Islesboro only to discover there wasn't much to see, the little village at Dark Harbor, modest homes of local residents, and small summer camps. The opulent estates of the rich, nestled in choice sites along the convoluted shoreline, weren't visible from the two-lane highway, and, disappointingly, one could drive from one end of the island to the other and see only occasional glimpses of water.

In addition to these transient sightseers, the summer residents who didn't participate in the co-op usually dropped in to browse from time to time, especially when they had guests. Then there were the wealthy treasure seekers, like this woman with the foghorn voice and her friend, hard put to find something special enough upon which to spend their money. Likely as not, they had driven over from Bar Harbor that morning.

"I'll take this sampler and that tapestry. Helen wants the infant pillow cover. While you wrap them up, we'll look around some more."

Swept by the familiar ambivalence, Jane didn't know whether to be happy or depressed. The two women had selected several of her choice and most expensive pieces, including the Garden of Eden tapestry, eighteen by twenty-four inches of solid embroidery. It had taken her months. She'd gotten her inspiration from an illustration in an old Bible that had belonged to the sea captain Patton who had amassed the original Patton fortune.

Everyone who had ever seen the hanging had admired it, but Jane had priced it high, not just because of the labor involved, she realized now, but because she hated to part with it. Still, the total amount of the sale was more than she'd ever earned in a single day.

"You should charge more for work like this," the woman boomed hoarsely as she leaned over toward Jane, attempting to offer her advice in confidence. Jane almost chuckled at the ludicrous situation as the woman and Helen paid for their purchases and prepared to take their leave, having found nothing else to tempt them.

Helen held back when her companion charged for the door. Her smile held a hint of apology that took Jane by surprise. "Have you ever thought of selling some of your designs to a manufacturer to be made into kits, especially the simpler ones? Ethel and I have friends that love to do needlework like this and would love to be able to work on designs like these. Yours are so original."

Jane had to restrain herself from hugging the woman, not just because of her compliment, but because she was the kind of person, after all, who could be trusted as a "guardian" of the lovely little satin cover for an infant's pillow that she had bought. It was embroidered with tiny comic animals. When Jane was working on it, she had explored the fantasy of having a child of her own someday, and tenderness had gone into each stitch.

"No, actually I haven't thought of doing that," Jane admitted warmly. But the idea stuck in her head, and she found herself mulling it over after the two women had gone. Wouldn't it be just too good to be true if she *did* prove to have a marketable skill after all, when certainly she hadn't been educated to earn a living? There hadn't seemed the remotest possibility that she would ever have to.

Then six years ago financial disaster had struck, and Lottie's fortune had been reduced to almost nothing.

Even then Jane had not been forced out into the working world. Lottie had sold her houses in Boston and Palm Beach, but kept the Islesboro cottage because Terry loved it. Jane had dropped out of college, convinced a very humble Terry that she still wanted to marry him, and then joined him and Lottie, her benefactor and now her mother-in-law, in what amounted to exile. They lived in the section of the huge summer mansion that had been winterized a year earlier for Terry's use when he came home from Paris, where he'd been studying and painting for the better part of the past three years. Suddenly there were no servants, no trips to Paris for clothes, no huge dinner parties. Life had been stripped to the essentials.

Jane had no regrets for the choices she had made six years ago. In no way did she feel a martyr. But the undercurrent of excitement churning inside her was more than just the simple joy that spring had come. *She was ready for a change.* It had been a whole year now since Terry hadn't been able to fight off that bout of pneumonia. He was gone. There was no reason she and Lottie should stay on at Islesboro, two women alone, enduring the long, harsh winters. The cottage was much too large for them, and it was getting more rundown every year. Even if it had always been in the Patton family, the only sensible thing to do was to sell it. Jane's only problem was convincing Lottie Patton of that fact.

She worked through the noon hour and then returned to the cottage, having finished her tour of duty at the co-op for the day. Lottie wouldn't have eaten lunch. It was Jane's own fault for pampering her, but the older woman still hadn't learned to do for herself.

As she turned the huge old Lincoln into the overgrown entrance of the lane that wound through several wooded acres back to the cottage, Jane saw in her mind the way the entrance once had been when there had been gardeners to maintain the beautiful landscaping. Now there was a jungle of unpruned shrubbery and rosebushes left to grow wild. She probably wouldn't be so keenly conscious of the neglect if she hadn't talked to a realtor recently about the possibility of putting the cottage up for sale. Since then she had been seeing the entire estate with painfully clear vision, the way she thought a stranger might see it.

Rounding a final curve, she knew the precise instant the thirty-room "cottage" would loom into view. Once a pristine white, it quite noticeably needed painting, but even more serious than that cosmetic defect were the leaks that had begun to open up in the enormous red tile roof. Those would quickly result in structural deterioration if left unrepaired. Jane shuddered to think what expense such repairs would entail, certainly more than she and Lottie could afford. It was a relief to think of some new owner shouldering the responsibility.

Yes, they definitely had to sell the cottage. Today she would approach the matter again with Lottie, more firmly this time.

She parked the aging hulk of an automobile at the right end of the cottage and walked around to the back. Just as she expected, Lottie was sitting on the terrace in the full sunshine, playing solitaire, seemingly oblivious to the soul-stirring vista of Penobscot Bay she had only to lift her head to see.

Jane stood at the corner of the cottage a moment, looking at the familiar scene with dual vision, seeing it the way it was now and the way it *had* been. The rear grounds of the estate were extensive and had once been Lottie's pride when she could afford to employ the staff of gardeners it had taken to maintain the elaborate landscaping. Now the shrubbery was untended and the many flowerbeds allowed to flourish on their own with weeds and die-hard perennials that came up each year. Jane planted a few marigolds and geraniums in the beds flanking the terrace, but she couldn't hope to take care of the whole place. Abe Johnson, who also supplied their firewood for the fireplaces, came every few weeks during the summer and mowed the grass.

Jane knew that a prospective buyer for the place would look at the terrace and reflect that it was very large and almost bare. She could easily conjure up in her mind the way it had looked in those days when Lottie would have a fancy luncheon or cocktail party for fifty guests. The gleaming white wicker furniture of those former days was reduced now to a few lounge chairs scattered here and there and one round table with four chairs, the table at which Lottie now sat, playing cards. The rest of the furniture was either stored away, in need of repairs, or long since discarded.

At least the view from the terrace had not changed with time. It had its own grandeur, whatever the time of day or night, whatever the season of the year. Jane loved those eerie mornings when the bay would be wreathed in veils of fog and she couldn't see where the rear lawn ended and the icy blue water began. But then, she also exulted in the sense of vastness one felt on a brilliantly clear day like today, when Penobscot Bay glittered like a huge sapphire and islands in the distance were green velvet mounds, while over to the right on the mainland were the emerald hills of Camden. If Jane were to leave Islesboro tomorrow and never return, she would always carry the un-spoiled beauty of this scenery with her in her heart and mind.

The reflection brought poignancy to her breast and a pensive note to her voice as she called out to alert Lottie to her presence in case she hadn't heard the car.

"I'm back."

The woman seated on the terrace was in her mid-fifties. Jane could remember her the way she once had been, too, the empress of her empire. Today, thank God, Lottie looked more like her old self, a sign Jane wished to interpret as hope that Lottie was healing inside. Terry's death had devastated her, taking away her own will to live. But with the coming of spring, she had begun to pay attention to her grooming again. Attired in a rose silk dressing gown, she was wearing makeup, and her pale blond hair was sprayed stiffly into place. Her head had just a hint of the old imperious carriage.

Jane knew that a closer inspection of the silk dressing gown would show that it had seen better days. It was stained and fraying around the seams, but it had been of superb quality, purchased in those days when only the best would do. Lottie's coiffure wasn't really up to the old standard, either, but Jane did her best. She had learned to color it and was absolutely insistent that it be kept up, even in those blackest days when Lottie hadn't really cared if she lived or died, arose from her bed or just lay there. It had become almost an obsession with Jane during that period to maintain as best she could Lottie's grooming, which had always been of great importance to her. What she was really hoping to do, of course, was to keep Lottie intact somehow. Today she could almost tell herself that she had succeeded.

Lottie glanced up at the sound of Jane's voice, and her hands stopped in mid-motion, beams of sunlight glancing off the facets of the diamonds in her wedding rings, which she hadn't parted with along with most of the rest of her fabulous jewelry collection.

"Hello, Jane, dear. What information did you glean from the local Islesboro citizenry today? Surely there was talk of the weather."

The faint note of condescension, which was welcome to Jane's ears, another sign of normalcy, was mixed with a restrained eagerness that was puzzling. And nothing usually interfered with Lottie's solitaire game, certainly not a routine inquiry into Jane's day. She played it automatically and almost continuously from waking to sleeping, often even while she watched television. It had occurred to Jane that for Lottie, a pack of cards served well as a substitute for a string of prayer beads.

"You can be sure that the topic of the weather was well covered," Jane replied cheerfully, continuing the distance to the terrace and coming to a standstill at the table. She didn't sit down because she intended to go inside and prepare a late lunch for the two of them.

To her amazement, Lottie's hands remained idle, and up close it was even more evident to Jane that her mother-in-law was excited about something. "What . . ." she began, and then followed Lottie's gaze as the older woman looked over to the left, where the curvature of the coastline made it possible to see the cottage on the adjoining estate, built in the early 1920s by the same Patton who had built this cottage a few years later for his son as a wedding present.

Now Jane knew what Lottie was worked up about. In Jane's absence that morning, a network of scaffolding had been constructed and a crew of painters were busily at work. Their progress wasn't discernible from this distance since they were painting white on white and James's cottage hadn't been allowed to go without regular upkeep like this one. His grandfather, whom Jane thought of always as Old Mr. Patton, had opened the cottage each summer for his own use until three years ago, when he died.

In addition to the painters, there was a small army of other workers visible around the grounds, an indication to Jane, and obviously to Lottie, too, that more than just routine maintenance was in progress next door. The cottage was being readied for occupancy.

Jane sat down abruptly at the table, her thoughts scattered. *Was James coming back here to Islesboro after all these years?* They hadn't seen him or heard from him in the past six years. He had seemed to be keeping his bitter promise of never bothering any of them again. A much more likely explanation was that he had offered the cottage to friends.

"I forgot to mention yesterday that I ran into Estelle Johnson at the drugstore," Jane murmured thoughtfully. "She said Abe wouldn't have time to spare for us this summer." Abe Johnson had always worked for Old Mr. Patton during the summers. "She said their grandson, Bobby, would be happy to come every two weeks and cut the lawn. He's saving money to go to college." Jane planned to have Bobby do some pruning, too, and help her weed the flowerbeds. She intended to do her best to make the cottage grounds presentable to the eyes of a potential buyer.

Lottie had absently begun to play cards again, but her attention was obviously still on the activity in progress on the adjoining estate. Now that her own initial surprise had faded, Jane wondered what was going on in her mother-in-law's mind. There had never been any love lost between Lottie and her nephew, James. Surely Lottie hadn't forgotten that James hadn't even come to Terry's funeral or sent any message of condolence. Jane would probably have thought less of him if he had. Whatever one could say of James, he had never been a hypocrite.

"I'll make us some lunch. I don't know about you, but I'm starving." Jane got up from the table, glad to postpone the discussion ahead. After they had eaten, she would bring up the subject of selling the cottage, and, at that time, erase any futile hopes Lottie might be harboring about James coming to their rescue at this late date.

Jane entered the cottage through French doors that stood open, and passed through the dining room, a huge high-ceilinged room she remembered as the scene of elegant dinner parties, the ladies in French gowns and jewels and the men in white dinner jackets. The jewel-toned Oriental rug had been custom-loomed to the dimensions of the room, the gilt mirror over the mantel imported from France for that very spot. Jane hoped to convince Lottie to let the rug and the mirror go with the cottage to enhance its value. They were both much too large for an ordinary house, apartment, or condominium.

From the dining room she entered a hallway that led to the kitchen, built and equipped on the scale of a restaurant's kitchen. There a chef had reigned over a staff of underlings in those opulent years when the Pattons played host during the summer to titled guests from foreign lands as well as to America's own untitled royalty. In the center of the room was an iron and porcelain monster of a stove that hopelessly intimidated Jane. Big iron hooks in the exposed beams overhead still held an array of heavy copper skillets, pots, and cooking implements, all dark with age and disuse. In one corner of the room were sinks as large as vats.

Jane bypassed the stove and went over to a marble counter that was her work center, with a few modern cooking appliances, including a toaster, a coffeemaker, an electric skillet, and a hot plate with two burners. While she heated a can of cream of mushroom soup and put together a tuna salad, Jane thought about the history of the Patton family, reflecting that it would be well-suited for one of those sweeping television sagas, at least until one got to the present. There the glamor faded into the stuff of reality that didn't entertain nearly so well as fables of wealth and power.

The James Patton who had begun the Patton shipping dynasty in the late 1800s started out as a ship's captain with more ambition and daring than capital. He died the owner of a large fleet of sailing ships, passing them on to his son, also named James, who displayed daring of a different kind, and guided the family business into the world of steam-powered vessels, multiplying the original fortune. This Patton had built the two summer mansions on Islesboro, one for himself and one for his son, Jonathan, whom Jane had known as Old Mr. Patton. She remembered him vividly as a stern man with a clipped gray beard and fierce dark eyes whose gaze she had been unable to hold for more than a second or two. Actually she had seen him only a few times, since he and Lottie did not get along.

He had sired twin sons, neither of whom Jane had known, though she had seen pictures of them. Both Terry's father and James's father were dead by the time Lottie took in Jane and her mother when Jane was ten. Terry's father had been a hopeless alcoholic and had died in a sanitorium abroad. James's father and mother had been killed in a plane crash when James was eight years old, leaving Old Mr. Patton to rear James, a duty he thought Lottie should assume, not him. Her failure to do so strengthened the animosity between them. According to Lottie, her father-in-law blamed her for her husband's alcoholism.

Jane had always thought it unfair of him to extend his dislike of Lottie to Terry, who was a Patton by blood and every bit as much the old man's grandson as James was. He had never relented though. When Lottie had lost most of her money, Old Mr. Patton hadn't offered to help. He'd continued to come to Islesboro each summer and had ignored them. When he died he didn't leave Terry a cent in his will. Presumably James had inherited everything and had not seen fit to right his grandfather's wrong.

"You should have sent me to a good cooking school instead of to that fancy finishing school, Aunt Lottie," Jane joked lightly as she served the simple lunch out on the terrace.

"The salad looks very tempting, dear." Lottie's remark was typically evasive. Even after six years she still could not bring herself to speak openly about her financial circumstances. Although it happened less and less, she still occasionally tried to foster the illusion that they *would* have someone in to do the cleaning and the laundry if only good help were available. Jane had finally begun to realize that she hadn't done Lottie any good by not forcing her to come to terms with reality.

"At least my background is good for something," she said now, with good-natured irony. "I may not know how to cook, but I do know the art of garnishing."

They ate in silence for several minutes. Jane was so busy with her own thoughts, mentally working up her courage to introduce the subject of putting the cottage up for sale, that Lottie's unexpected remarks took a few moments to sink in.

"Won't it be nice if James does open the cottage this summer. He'll probably be inviting guests, having parties . . ." Lottie swept Jane a guileless glance. "James was always very fond of you, wasn't he?" Before Jane could recover from her amazement, the older woman was continuing, a frown creasing her forehead. "We really must get someone in to help. The patio furniture must be gotten out of storage, cleaned, and painted. The terrace awning . . . oh, but it is too badly ripped to be mended, isn't it? You never had another one made, did you, Jane?"

"No, Aunt Lottie!" Jane retorted sharply. "I *didn't* have another awning made for the terrace! You know good and well we don't have the money for things like that!" She checked herself and continued in a calmer but nonetheless firm tone. "If James does come here this summer, it isn't likely he'll be inviting either of us to his parties, and even if he did, we couldn't possibly hope to reciprocate." Jane noted with compunction the hurt on her mother-in-law's face. But Lottie was going to have to face up to reality.

"I suppose you're right," Lottie murmured. "I'm so sorry, dear. Believe me, I wanted so much more for you. . . ."

Jane swallowed hard and steeled herself not to give in to her pity. "I know you did, Aunt Lottie," she said gently. "Goodness knows you've been good to me, treated me like your own daughter, given me everything when you had it to give. But it won't help matters to pretend that everything's the way it used to be. We've got to live in the present." Jane could tell from the vagueness settling over Lottie's features that the older woman was retreating, tuning out what she didn't want to hear.

"Aunt Lottie, listen to me!" Jane ordered sharply. "I've talked to a real estate agent about selling the cottage. He thinks we should be able to get a good price for it if we can find the right buyer. It's just too big for us. It's too much for us to keep up."

The expression in Lottie's eyes denounced Jane for an ingrate and a traitor, but at least it wasn't vague. "Sell the cottage," she echoed. "Sell my *home*, all that I have left . . ." Her voice gained strength, became infused with accusation and a touch of the old arrogance. "How on earth can you suggest such a thing? This cottage has always been in the Patton family." The spurt of defiance faded as quickly as it had risen, leaving her crushed and defenseless. "Terry loved this place," she whispered. "He spent the last years of his life here. Doesn't that *mean* anything to you, Jane?"

Jane had to reach deep inside herself for strength. Was she wrong in trying to force Lottie to sell the cottage? Was it Lottie's destiny to stay here on Islesboro, where she had retired from the outside world? But what about Jane's destiny, which was linked with Lottie's?

"Yes, Aunt Lottie, all of that *does* mean something to me," Jane said quietly. "But Terry's gone now, and *we're* alive. We've got to do what's best for *us*."

Lottie presented no further argument. Jane would have liked to believe that the issue was settled, but she knew that it wasn't. In the meanwhile she would proceed without Lottie's actual permission, trusting that when the time came, she would get Lottie to place her signature on the necessary contracts.

As she cleared away the lunch dishes, Jane thought of that remark of Lottie's a few minutes ago that she hadn't addressed. *James was always very fond of you, wasn't he?* What an odd and totally unexpected thing for Lottie to say, especially in that tone of voice that, in retrospect, had been almost knowing. Jane had never told Lottie of any of those old incidents that were more ripples of sensation now than actual recollections. The first time James had gotten her alone and forced his sexual attentions upon her, she had been only thirteen and too embarrassed to tell anyone what had happened, although he had actually only kissed her and touched her ripening breasts.

In later years the encounters had grown less innocent, with James using his superior strength to take more intimate liberties, but still she had never told anyone, not even Terry after she and Terry had become unofficially engaged. It was as though by her earlier silence she had allowed herself to be drawn into a guilty complicity with James, her arch foe.

Even now Jane didn't choose to dwell upon those memories, though she better understood the sense of shame for what it had been. James had been able to arouse her in spite of her opposition, and she had felt degraded by her unwilling response. He had thrown it up to her when she turned down his proposal, demanding to know how she could marry one man when she was turned on by another. Jane had come back with the scathing answer, "You don't want to marry me, James! You just don't want Terry to have me."

And it had been the truth. James had simply been obeying that old compulsion to best Terry at everything. He would actually have married Jane to prove that he could take his cousin's fiancée away from him!

Jane shook her head even now, remembering. Then she put it all out of her mind. It was ancient history and had no importance in her life now—nor in James's, she was sure.

Chapter Two

I say, James, old man, do you make a habit of spying on your neighbors with binoculars," Anthony Bursford teased in his dry British accent.

"It's probably an old flame from his youth," Belinda accused, pouting. "Here, let me see."

James ignored both of them. He was almost oblivious to their presence in the large cockpit of the yacht that swung gently at its mooring some yards from shore. Only dimly did he hear the shouts and laughter and sounds of splashing coming from the water. His patience had been rewarded. Jane had emerged onto the terrace. He wasn't prepared for the lurch in his chest or the sudden rush of blood through his veins. God, he hadn't known he would react like this on seeing her again. He had thought he had put it all behind him. In the back of his mind, coming up here again had been a kind of test.

She hadn't changed at all. The unruly dark brown hair with its glints of mahogany was gathered up into a topknot. Curly wisps had escaped around her face and neck. Memory aided the powerful lenses of the binoculars to bring into focus the vulnerability of her face: clear hazel eyes, soft lips that betrayed every emotion, sensitive skin that burned and freckled but didn't tan.

She still had that deceptively fragile look, her breasts seeming a little too large on her slight build. James knew from experience that she was actually quite strong and well-coordinated. He remembered her across the net from him on the tennis court, her face set with determination. He remembered her stroking furiously through the icy bay water beside him until he put on a burst of speed and left her behind. He remembered the feel of her as she'd struggled in his forced embrace.

God, he remembered . . . he remembered. What a fool he'd been to come back, but he had to see her up close now, if only to conquer the demon of memory.

Without a word James got up and went down inside the yacht, where he put the binoculars away. He didn't want Belinda or any of the others to be looking on when he encountered Jane face to face for the first time in six years. Outside, still ignoring the curious faces and teasing gibes, he poised on the rail and dived cleanly into the water, absorbing the shock of its coldness.

Jane saw the large black-hulled sloop the moment she walked through the French doors onto the terrace. Its presence just offshore from James's property was in no way unusual this time of year. James had probably given someone permission to use his mooring. Penobscot Bay, with its hundreds of islands, was a favorite summer cruising ground with yachtsmen.

She shivered involuntarily as a figure dived from the deck of the yacht into the bay. It was a lovely June day, but she knew well how cold the water would be. Even in the middle of July the bay was cold. Jane had a sudden disconcerting memory of her first experience of its frigid temperature. It was one of those early times when she had been duped by James. She remembered the shock of the water hitting her body, the sound of James's laughter, the chatter of her teeth as she forced her numb limbs into movement, determined that she would stay in the water even if she did turn to ice.

Shrugging aside the memory, Jane set about the task at hand, forcing herself not to think of the collective hours of work it would take to weed *all* the flowerbeds. She'd take them one at a time. It was the same mental attitude she was adopting toward putting the cottage up for sale. Yesterday she'd gone to the realtor's office and begun the paperwork. The next step was getting Lottie's signature on the listing contract along with her own.

In the meanwhile, Jane was doing everything she could to make the cottage and grounds presentable. The Johnson boy was taking care of cutting the grass and had also agreed to do some pruning with Jane's less-than-expert supervision, but she was fully capable of weeding the flowerbeds and setting out marigold and geranium plants to add to the brave floral display of those hardy perennials that sprang up each year.

Her inclination was to start at those beds nearest the terrace, the ones she tended after a fashion each spring, but those farther down, nearer the bay, were more neglected. She'd do well to work on them while she was fresh.

Gardening was not Jane's passion, especially not on such a large scale, but the sun was warm on her back as she crouched on her knees and attacked the weeds in the bed she'd chosen. The sea gulls and crows down along the shore were carrying on a raucous argument. It was pleasant to be outside, and she had enough to think about to take her mind off the tedium of her task.

Once they had sold the cottage, where would she and Lottie live? They should have enough money to buy a small house. Jane thought she would like to move to a warm climate, just for the change. Jane would get a job—doing *something*. Vague as the plan was, it excited her. Lottie would still have her small income from what remained of her investments. Hopefully, in a totally new setting, Lottie would become interested in living again, make friends, go shopping—do all those normal things she had given up the past six years.

Lost in her pleasant speculations about the future, Jane leaned forward, her back to the bay, and launched a ferocious attack on the weeds in the middle of the large bed that bordered one side of an area of lawn where she and Terry had spent many hours as children playing croquet. She didn't actually hear footsteps or feel their vibration, but something suddenly alerted her to the presence of another person. There was a moment of inexplicable panic, as though danger were near, perhaps because Jane had her back to the bay and no one should be moving up behind her from that direction.

Drawing in her breath, she straightened the upper

part of her body quickly and looked around, still on her knees. At the totally unexpected sight of the man approaching, her eyes widened and her already rapid heartbeat accelerated to a pace that made her light-headed for a split-second.

James! Coming right up out of the bay, his dark hair sleek against his skull, his compact, muscular body dripping water, the thin black tank suit like a darker patch of skin. He was an apparition out of the past!

Jane sank back on her heels, coming quickly to her senses as she noted the differences as well as the similarities between the mature man who approached her and the fifteen-year-old boy who had made his entry into her life in precisely this same way. This was the present-day James, not the ghost of her old tormentor. Still hard and fit and totally in command of his body, always the natural athlete, he was nonetheless older, more controlled, the assurance real, not a brash pretense. His dark eyes held curiosity as they had that first time he'd inspected her, but now they were carefully guarded to conceal whatever else he might be feeling.

James hadn't meant to frighten her, as he so obviously had. He should have called out as soon as he waded up out of the water, but the sight of the place as well as Jane's occupation had taken him aback. He hadn't expected it to be so rundown nor her to be doing the work of a gardener. Before he could collect himself enough to speak, she had some-how sensed his presence and looked around.

The feeling of *déjà vu* closed in upon James as he walked nearer. He might have been fifteen again and seeing Jane for the first time. Dear God, could she really be looking at him with that same expression, a mixture of fear and defiance, as though she really would like nothing more than to run from the menace that had risen up right out of the icy sea. What was worse, James had to fight hard against the identical clash of protectiveness and aggression that had battled in his breast when he was fifteen, totally alone, bored, and filled with a baffled anger that made him want to smash things. He kept himself too busy now to be bored; he had conquered the anger and come to terms with being alone.

"Hello, Jane. Sorry, I didn't mean to startle you." James dropped down to the grass several yards away from her before she could stand up, obeying an instinct to break the parallel between this meeting and that first one more than a decade and a half ago. He hadn't come back here to replay scenes out of his past. They had been painful enough living through the first time.

"James," she whispered, curiously relieved that he had sat down. Suddenly it was seeming so normal. He had swum over from the yacht. That had been James she had glimpsed diving into the water.

"For a moment there I thought I was seeing a ghost. I was ten years old again and looking around for a croquet mallet." Her tone was light and self-deprecating, but underneath she was still a little shaken. And self-conscious. James's eyes were as dark and acutely observant as she remembered, although lacking the devilish gleam of mockery. He was taking in every single detail of her untidy appearance. The old cotton skirt and blouse were faded; her face was shiny, without a speck of makeup; her hair was straggling down around her face and neck. Jane felt as unimpressive today as she had felt the first day he'd inspected her.

"I almost expected you to say, 'So you're the new poor relation,'" she quipped defensively, brandishing the old memory as she had the croquet mallet.

James realized that he had been staring at her, as drawn to her as he had ever been and as unable to pinpoint exactly what it was about her that made her special. Certainly not beauty by conventional standards. He had dated his share of beautiful women with perfect figures, and none of them had ever touched him like Jane, an irony indeed since, literally speaking, she'd never voluntarily touched him at all, except in anger, after he had taunted her into loss of control. He'd done that the very first time he'd ever seen her. How well he remembered the way her eyes, huge in her thin face, had shot honey sparks of frustrated rage. Her bottom lip had been caught between her teeth to fight its tremors as she came at him with a croquet mallet.

He'd felt a surge of adrenaline, total mastery of the situation—and regret for the necessity of having to play the bully in order to be there at all. Not that he would have admitted at that time, even to himself, that what he really wanted was to be *included*.

Now that he had seen her again close up and felt again the powerful pull upon his emotions that had become complicated with sexual awareness as she grew into adolescence, James was no nearer to understanding his own vulnerability than he had ever been. With Jane's quite transparent attempt to use the past to throw up a wall between them now, to remind James that he was still as much of an intruder as ever, he was tempted to carry matters no further. He should probably jump back into the bay, swim back to the boat, and write this whole thing off as a mistake. They could have the anchor up and be gone in fifteen minutes.

"I was a real diplomat that first day, wasn't I?" His dry, amused tone was so convincingly detached that he decided to stay a few minutes longer. It took some effort to pull his gaze away from Jane, but he was making her uncomfortable. Glancing around at the cottage and grounds once again, he was struck with that same sense of disbelief at the obvious neglect. "Of course, you have to realize I'd been hearing you referred to in those terms by the servants. It just kind of slipped out."

A partial truth. He'd been curious as hell to see the kid his aunt had taken in, but of course there hadn't been any invitation, not for James, the bully, who might hurt delicate little Terence. So James had swum over and found his cousin and Jane playing croquet. She'd been laughing when he walked up, taking them by surprise. They'd both turned around and looked at him as if he were some kind of savage. Naturally he hadn't wanted to disappoint them.

Jane was remembering the encounter too. She had been so timid and insecure and eager to please the woman who had given her and her recently widowed mother a home. "Aunt" Lottie, actually a distant cousin, had gently but firmly impressed upon Jane that Terence was of a "delicate" constitution, and Jane must look out for him and never encourage him to engage in strenuous activities that might prove harmful to his health.

Enter James, whose reputation had already preceded him. Looking back now, Jane had to wonder if the actual circumstances had warranted the terror she had experienced. Had James actually been a serious physical threat to Terry or herself, then or any time afterward? It had seemed to her during that first encounter that her whole future depended upon shielding Terry, who at thirteen was three years her senior.

James had willingly accepted her as a decoy, taunting her into a violence of which she hadn't dreamed herself capable. A thin ten-year-old, she had stood her ground even though James at fifteen had the physique of a man. When words failed she had tried to hit him over the head with her croquet mallet. What blind fury had possessed her? What total frustration as James deftly kept himself just beyond reach, delighted with her loss of control. Then as suddenly as he had appeared he had made his departure, the episode apparently having lost its element of entertainment. Jane was left sick and trembling.

"You never ever really intended to hurt us, did you? For some reason you enjoyed terrorizing us, and then you'd get bored and walk away." Jane voiced the insight as it took place in her mind, her tone more interested than accusing.

James shrugged, choosing to acquiesce rather than to explain, although there had been more than simple pleasure in his urge to torment and certainly more than boredom behind his withdrawals. He glanced around, noting once again the neglected state of the cottage and the grounds, and then letting his gaze settle upon Jane, whose gloved hand still clutched the trowel.

"My aunt certainly has let this place go to hell. She

has you doing the yard work these days?" Try as he might, James couldn't keep his voice clear of a hint of the old contempt, and its effect on Jane was automatic. Immediately she rose to Lottie's defense.

"I don't know what you expected her to do on her income! And she doesn't *have* me doing anything I don't want to do," Jane informed him scornfully, rising up on her knees, her hands planted firmly on her hips. The defiant posture thrust her breasts forward, and she felt her face grow hot as James's dark eyes went over her quite thoroughly once again. It only added to her fury that he could make her so intensely conscious of her body!

Her anger stimulated him the way it always had. He wanted to stoke it, make it burn higher, out of control. *God, he was aching to touch her.* What strange madness was this that still claimed him?

Jane had been tensed in expectation of a quick, deadly reply. When moments passed and James said nothing, she felt a little foolish and settled back on her haunches again, the relaxation of her posture an admission that her reaction had been stronger than was warranted.

"I knew, of course, that my aunt's business affairs had been mismanaged," James said carefully, "that she had suffered some substantial losses and had to sell the houses in Boston and Palm Beach, but I had no idea . . ." His frown rested upon the trowel Jane clutched before sweeping once more over the cottage and grounds. "You're not saying that she—the two of you—are *poor?*"

Surprise that he really seemed not to know, as well as his evident awkwardness at inquiring into their financial circumstances, kept Jane from being as of-

fended as she might otherwise have been. Still, it was
anything but easy telling James the truth and impossible not to be defensive.

"We're not paupers or wards of the state, but we
definitely can't afford to keep this place up. It's much
too big for us anyway." It had been impractical for
them to keep the cottage in the first place, but she had
no intention of discussing their reasons with James.
The possibility that he might voice some opinion on
the matter made her sound brusque as she continued.
"I've talked to a realtor. We'll be putting the cottage
up for sale soon."

He absorbed her revelation with a flash of surprise,
but her tone had effectively discouraged any spontaneous exclamations.

"My aunt has actually agreed to sell this place," he
mused skeptically, his dark eyes trained upon Jane's
features, which still hadn't learned how to lie. "She
hasn't, has she?" The harsh, knowing voice was
strangely at variance with his expressionless face.
Unlike Jane, James was a master at schooling his
features. "I didn't think so. After all, this is where her
beloved Terence chose to bury himself along with her
and you. She'll probably stay here—and keep you
with her—until the goddamned roof crumbles in on
your heads!" James was trembling inside by the time
he finished, the bitterness in his voice leaving an awful
taste in his mouth. His loss of control appalled him.
*And he had fooled himself into thinking he was over
the past.* Over the resentment and the jealousy and
the longing.

Jane had risen up on her knees again, her upper
torso stiffened with outrage. "You have no *right,*
James Patton! No right at all!" she blared at him. "It's

not your business what Lottie and I do! How *dare* you come back here and make judgments on us when you have *everything* and we have to face up to selling our *home!*" In the thick of battle there was no right or wrong, fair or unfair. Jane was fighting back with nothing but indignation and pride. "You haven't changed a bit, have you, James?"

She hurled the accusation, knowing full well she had never been able to make a dent upon James's composure with words. He had always deflected them like a smooth, hard stone bouncing back bullets. *But this time was different!* Jane drew in her breath in a shocked gasp as James came up into a low crouch and moved across the distance separating them, his face no longer controlled. His dark eyes burned with a light that frightened her with its awful intensity. His smile mocked himself as well as her.

"How right you are, Jane," he said softly, reaching her and dropping down to his knees in front of her. "I haven't changed a bit in some ways."

He rocked back a little, resting his hands on his muscular thighs, indolent and powerfully male, naked except for the brief black bathing suit that failed to conceal his virility. The very ease of his posture was a statement of dominance Jane was helpless to contradict.

"James, you can't do this!" she protested, fighting to wrest her gaze away from the burning darkness of his eyes with their blatant intention.

"Can't do what, Jane?" he mocked softly. "I haven't done anything yet. And whenever I do, we both know you'll fight in spite of the fact that you'll like it as much as I do."

"Don't be ridiculous! I *never* liked . . . *anything*

you did to me!" She turned her head sideways so that she couldn't see him, and yet her senses were filled with his intoxicating closeness. She held her breath, waiting.

"Why did you always fight, Jane?" he was murmuring, nearer now. She could feel his breath against her neck, and the suspense was excruciating. "You know you like the feel of my hands touching you . . ." Jane sucked in sharply as his fingers cupped her breasts, teasing, so that she could just barely feel the contact, and yet the response of her body was immediate. Her breasts rounded and grew heavier, the nipples contracting.

"James!" His thumbs had flicked lightly over the hard peaks.

"You like it, Jane. You like this too," he whispered, and then she felt his breath scorching her neck an instant before his lips were sliding along the sensitive curve, rediscovering the plundered territory. When Jane finally made a move and tried to pull away, James's arms closed around her, ending the playful devastation.

"Why do you go through this charade and fight me, Jane?" he was demanding hoarsely. "Do you want me to *force* you? You know I want you, and I'd do anything to please you."

Not waiting for an answer, James took her head in both his hands and captured her lips in a hard, demanding kiss that went on so long, her lungs were aching for oxygen. When she gasped for air, he made a low sound of satisfaction and sent his tongue plunging into her mouth. Jane twisted and pushed him away.

"Why do you like it like this, Jane?" he murmured

against her lips and pushed her back on the ground, pinning her with his hard, heavy length. Capturing both of her wrists, he held her arms out to each side and waited, as though for a reply.

"I *don't* like it—" Jane muttered between her teeth, struggling more to emphasize her denial than with any hope of eluding him. When he slowly lowered his head toward her chest, she went still but kept her back arched. Even through the fabric of her blouse and the bra underneath it, the warmth and suction of his mouth on the hard peak of her breast was delicious torment. Jane moaned softly. James moved over to the other breast then, but only for long enough to sharpen the ache deep in her abdomen. Then he was raising his head and looking into her face, which must, she knew, be telling him everything his male ego demanded to know.

"Tell me you like me to do that, Jane," he demanded softly, moving his hips against hers so that she could feel the hard thrust of his arousal. Pure instinct made Jane want to open her thighs and accommodate the contact.

"Why don't you just go ahead and rape me, James?" Her voice was thin with desperation.

To Jane's surprise an expression of disappointment flickered across James's face before it hardened, the hazy passion all gone.

"You'd like that, wouldn't you?" he said harshly, lifting his hips and ramming hard into her in a parody of the violent invasion she'd suggested. "That way you could have me make love to you without any complicity on your part, without losing pride or breaking old loyalties. But I have no intention of forcing my way inside you, Jane. I could have had you like that years ago." He released her hands and raised himself up slowly, taking the hard weight of his body away from hers, but holding her with his intense gaze. "You're going to have to admit you want me. I *swear* you're going to do that someday." His face became hazy with passion again as he looked at her lying there. "When we do make love, Jane, you're going to know what it's like to be a woman, *my* woman," he said softly, and reached out to trace her feminine triangle with the tips of his fingers.

Jane finally moved, then, reacting to the bolt of sensation that shot through her. She came upright and then stood up on legs that threatened to wobble. Before she could muster her composure enough to speak, James was leaving as abruptly as he had arrived.

"James!" She was wasting her breath. He was already halfway down to the water and didn't even look back. "Of all the *nerve!*" Jane muttered helplessly, watching James as he reached the water's edge, waded out some yards, and then plunged headfirst. With grudging admiration she noted the power and yet the consummate grace of his strokes as he swam back toward the black-hulled yacht. James had always made swimming look so effortless.

She watched him until he had almost reached the yacht, and then she turned her back to the bay, not wanting James to see her standing there, gazing after him. All interest in weeding the flowerbed had definitely vanished, but she retrieved her trowel and knelt down again, attacking the weeds absently while she played the whole amazing scene over in her mind.

To have James appear after six years of absence and silence was amazing enough in itself, but who would have expected her to end up in his arms again, the object of his sexual harassment? *Harassment . . . was that a fair assessment of what had happened?* Jane couldn't honestly assure herself that it was. James had accused her today of putting up a resistance that was only token since she actually wanted the intimacy he forced upon her.

Could that possibly be true? Jane's first instinct was to reject the notion, but closing her eyes, she let herself recapture the feel of his hands lightly cupping her breasts, the brush of his lips along her neck, the hard thrust of his contours against the cradle of her pelvis. The memory quickened her breathing and stirred to life sensations that bore no resemblance to disgust. Opening her eyes again, Jane admitted the truth. She had *not* been repelled by James's touch, not today.

Actually there had *never* been any physical revulsion, a fact perhaps that had made Jane fight even harder when James took her into his arms. It had deepened her shame to know that she could be aroused on a purely animal level by a man she didn't like, *even after she and Terry were engaged to be married!*

But Jane wasn't buying James's accusation that she had always secretly wanted him to take her by force. That simply was not true.

The old sexual tension had been there between them the moment James walked up. Jane had resisted it—*and* James—automatically. She didn't know why, probably just from the habit of years. Now that Terry was gone, there would be no breach of loyalty if she allowed herself to respond to James sexually, would there?

Uneasy with her whole train of thought, Jane reminded herself that such speculation had little purpose. James had come, and he had gone. Probably she wouldn't see him again for another six years, possibly not *ever* again.

Oddly hesitant at verifying her intuition, Jane looked around over her shoulder toward the spot where the yacht had swung at its mooring. Just as she had expected, it was gone.

Chapter Three

Jane waited until after supper that evening to tell Lottie that James had been there, and then she made the revelation casually.

"James was here this afternoon."

They were sitting in the big main parlor, which they could use now that it was summer. In the winter they used a smaller sitting room that was heated. Even in June the fire Jane had built in the fireplace felt good, and it added a sense of tranquility.

Lottie was watching television. When she said nothing, Jane looked up from her needlework, a very intricate new cross-stitch design, to make sure her mother-in-law had heard. It was then that Jane realized the impact of her offhanded announcement on the older woman. The eagerness with which Lottie was awaiting for further details was disquieting. *Surely Lottie didn't expect anything from James.*

"He swam over from a yacht." Jane tried to sound as though having James drop by was nothing out of the ordinary. "He stayed just a few minutes and swam back. Then the yacht left." It was difficult not to pause here as her nerves tightened. "I told him we planned to put the cottage up for sale. Which reminds me—Mr. Blockett will be bringing by some papers for us to sign."

"You *told* James we were selling the cottage. What on earth did he say?"

The strange combination of outrage and desperation made Jane's skin crawl. For just a second her courage wavered. Cruelty for the sake of kindness was easier to embrace in principle than it was to enact.

"He was surprised, but actually he had little to say." Quite literally, that was true. What he had said Jane didn't intend to repeat. She steeled herself to snip a thread of hope as fine as gossamer. "One might have thought some feeling of family loyalty would make James want to do anything to keep this place from falling into the hands of strangers—why, he could buy it himself—but obviously Patton tradition means little to him. But then, so far as we know, anyway, James has never married. He's what—thirty-two by now. Maybe he doesn't plan to ever have any children to pass these cottages on to."

Jane looked down quickly, blindly stabbing the needle into fabric and feeling a sharp twinge of compassion in her breast. Her instincts had been right. Unlikely as it seemed, Lottie *had* been clinging to some totally unfounded hope that the nephew for whom she had never shown the slightest affection would now in the hour of need come to her aid. *The black knight of old mounted upon a white steed.*

A bizarre and disturbing vision flashed into Jane's mind—James as he had looked hours earlier that day, supple and brown and wet, wearing nothing but that revealing black nylon swimsuit, but mounted on a white war horse. A little shiver went over the whole surface of her skin. Guiltily Jane glanced up at Lottie, whom she had quite forgotten for a second or two, caught up in the sheer eroticism of her imaginings. What had gotten into her today?

Her mother-in-law was gazing at the television screen, but Jane didn't think that she was actually seeing it. It hurt to see her look so apathetic. Jane had to remind herself of that rosy future she had contemplated for the two of them that afternoon, before James had arrived. Moving would be painful for Lottie, but beneficial in the long run.

"Mr. Blockett will be coming by either tomorrow or the next day with papers for us to sign. He's given me his word we won't be bothered with anyone who isn't a legitimate prospective buyer." Jane didn't feel nearly so casual as she sounded. Lottie hadn't reacted at all to the mention of the realtor earlier. Her attention had been taken totally with the fact of James's visit.

Jane watched the play of emotions on her mother-in-law's face and braced herself for yet another scene. The silence went on so long, she didn't think Lottie intended to speak at all.

"If I lose this place, I'll have nothing left . . . nothing . . ." Lottie finally murmured almost inaudibly.

James's contemptuous words about his aunt that afternoon were replayed in Jane's head: *She'll probably stay here—and keep you with her—until the goddamned roof crumbles in on your heads!* Now Jane answered not just her mother-in-law, but James as well.

"That's not true, Aunt Lottie." The denial was firm. "You have me. You have many wonderful memories." She hesitated. Lottie hadn't ventured inside Terry's studio so far as Jane knew during the year since he had died. "We both have Terry's paintings."

Lottie continued to stare at the television screen, giving no sign that she had heard Jane except for a little spasm of pain that crossed her features. When long minutes passed and she still made no reply, Jane simply didn't have the heart to persist with the conversation and try to get Lottie to admit that Jane's decision to sell the cottage was the only practical solution to their present financial problems. They couldn't stay here year after year, no matter what the sentimental attachments.

Jane concentrated on executing tiny, perfect stitches, and thought about the future. Perhaps she could get a job working in a shop that sold needlework supplies and kits. She might even teach various types of needlework, in connection with the hypothetical job—or even on her own. Glancing up now and then at Lottie, Jane had to stifle a little feeling of guilt that thoughts of a future in a different place so enticed her.

The realtor's excitement was evident at first glance. A portly man of medium height, Ted Blockett's thin rust-colored hair revealed his pink scalp. His complexion was made ruddy by the network of blood vessels close to the surface, and contrasted strongly to his keen blue eyes. For his mission today he wore a tweed jacket over his L. L. Bean plaid shirt and baggy twill pants.

Jane had gone to him because he lived on Islesboro himself, even though his main office was located on the mainland in Camden. He knew every piece of property on the island and had the reputation of finding buyers for specialized properties without wasting his time or the owner's with what he called "tire-kickers."

"I may have some good news," he told Jane with typical Maine restraint after she had greeted him at the front door and invited him in.

"Oh? What's that?" Jane felt as distracted as she sounded. Now that the first major hurdle had arrived —the moment when Lottie would have to put her signature on the realtor's contract, signifying her willingness to sell—Jane was nervous. There might be another grueling scene. Jane would just have to stand firm.

"It looks as though you may already have a buyer willing to pay the price we had discussed." Ted Blockett had told her quite honestly that figure was more than they could expect to get. He'd explained that an "asking price" should always leave room for bargaining.

"A *buyer* . . . but how could you already have a buyer?" Jane stared at him perplexedly. "We haven't even signed the contract yet. The cottage isn't actually for sale yet, is it?" She was thinking that things were happening too fast. It wouldn't do for Lottie to know there was already a buyer. The first step was getting her accustomed to the idea of offering the cottage for sale.

Jane's agitation wasn't lost on Ted Blockett. A

discreet expression settled over his features as he resolved to get things straight before he left here today. If the two Patton women were going to back out of selling, he'd rather they do it right now, when he hadn't really gone to any considerable amount of trouble on their behalf. He knew a little of the family history involved. In situations like this, one was apt to run into all sorts of eccentricity. A house this old and this large had God knows how many closets crammed full of skeletons.

"Not if you and your mother-in-law have changed your minds, it isn't," Ted replied politely, ready to climb back into his car and drive back to Camden. He wouldn't have been human not to be a mite disappointed, considering a buyer had dropped right into his lap. The Boston realtor hadn't divulged his client's name but had claimed he was a man of substantial means who had been interested in the Patton property for a number of years and had heard a rumor that it might be on the market.

"We haven't changed our minds," Jane replied quickly, wiping her palms along her skirt, a long-standing habit. "If you'll just leave the papers with me, I'll bring them to you tomorrow, signed."

"No reason for you to go to all that trouble, Mrs. Patton," Ted protested genially. "I'm not in a bit of a hurry." Not a particularly suspicious man by nature, Ted Blockett nonetheless wanted to see Lottie Patton sign the listing contract.

"Very well." Jane drew in a deep breath. "My mother-in-law is out on the terrace."

Ted was reassured when he stepped out on the sunny terrace and saw a well-groomed woman in her mid-fifties playing solitaire. She paused and acknowledged Jane's introduction with a regal nod of her head, but the hostility in her blue eyes put Ted once more on the alert. He didn't think Lottie Patton was hearing a word of his explanation of the terms in the listing contract. When he had finished, she held out her hand. After a slight hesitation he handed the document to her.

"Sir—" Her patronizing tone made it clear she was speaking to a social inferior. "My daughter-in-law has consulted you quite on her own and without my permission. I have no intention whatever of selling this cottage. It was built by my husband's grandfather and has always been in the Patton family. I am sorry you have needlessly been put to some trouble." She tore the contract into two pieces, fitted those together, and tore the half pages into quarters. Then she tossed the pieces aside, letting them flutter to the flagstone terrace, and resumed her solitaire game.

"Aunt Lottie—" Jane struggled to shake off the paralysis that was a devastating mixture of embarrassment, anger, and disappointment. She had been prepared for some resistance on her mother-in-law's part, but not for this arrogant performance!

"If you two ladies will excuse me . . ." Ted Blockett was making a polite little bow and then turning away to find his own way out now that his instincts had proved sound. Jane shot her mother-in-law an impotent glare and followed behind him. She was almost as angry at him as she was at Lottie.

"I told you to leave me the papers!" she gritted out between clenched teeth when they had both reached the front door and he had paused, aware that she was right on his heels.

"Mrs. Patton—"

"We're going to sell this cottage, Mr. Blockett!" Jane interrupted him shrilly. "If you don't want to handle it, some other real estate company will!"

After he had left, Jane was sorry she had spoken to him that way. None of what had happened had really been his fault. Who could blame him for not wanting to be involved?

Lottie wasn't on the terrace when Jane went back out there, steeled to do battle. She wasn't in any of the places where Jane looked. By the time Jane figured out where she was, her temper had cooled and mentally she backed off. Lottie had gone into Terry's studio, his sanctum where he had virtually lived and where he had drawn his last breaths. It was as though the older woman were looking to her dead son for support.

Jane had to wrestle with another attack of self-doubt. Was she right in trying to force Lottie to sell the cottage, leave Islesboro, and build a new life? *Yes.* She was certain that she was right. But what was she going to do if Lottie kept up this resistance? For the first time, Jane's confidence in being able to handle things wavered.

Ted Blockett wasted no time in telephoning the Boston realtor when he returned to his Camden office. Once he'd reported matter-of-factly the lack of accord between the two Patton women in regard to selling the Islesboro summer estate, he gave in to curiosity and pressed for more information on the interested buyer, now that the deal had fallen through. If the two women could come to an agreement to sell later on, Ted promised that the Boston realtor would be the first to know.

"Well I'll be," he said with mild surprise some moments later when the interested buyer's identity had been made known to him. "Don't that just beat all? 'Course there have been rumors about bad feelings in the Patton family for years, but you'd think close kin like a nephew—but then, rich folks don't always live by the same rules as the rest of us, do they, Joe?"

The next day Jane doggedly set about resuming her task of weeding the overgrown flowerbeds. To have abandoned her efforts at making the cottage grounds presentable would have seemed like giving in to Lottie, and she definitely *wasn't* giving in, no matter what tactics her mother-in-law used to wear down her determination. So far Lottie hadn't spoken a word to Jane or eaten a morsel of food following the scene with Ted Blockett.

As she relived that scene for the umpteenth time, Jane attacked the weeds ferociously, venting upon them her seething frustration. She could only hope that the unidentified buyer wouldn't lose interest in buying the estate during the time it would take Jane to make Lottie see reason. It was too good to be true that someone with the means to buy the cottage had appeared out of nowhere just at the right time, before the cottage was even advertised for sale. Aside from the realtor, Jane hadn't even mentioned to another outside person the possibility of selling the cottage . . . *except to James.*

Could James possibly be the unidentified buyer? Jane immediately rejected the thought. Why would James want his aunt's cottage when he had one of his own? Jane could think of only two possible motives, neither of them very likely. A strong sense of Patton tradition might make James want to keep the cottage in the family, or James might be willing to buy the estate just to help out Lottie and Jane. In either case, why would he go to a realtor instead of coming directly to Lottie and Jane? It didn't make sense.

No, the buyer wasn't James. He wasn't the surreptitious type. Who was it then? Someone perhaps who had been a guest in years past and remembered the Isleboro estate the way it was then? Someone who had known Lottie when she was a social lioness and didn't want to embarrass her now by declaring his—or her—identity?

So absorbed was she in her ruminations that Jane didn't hear the sound of an engine that she would have recognized as belonging to Abe Johnson's battered old pickup truck. She didn't realize she wasn't alone until the sound of a throat being cleared alerted her to the presence of other human beings. Looking up, she saw Abe and his grandson, Bobby, approaching her.

"Hello, Abe. Bobby. What can I do for you?" As she got to her feet, Jane was halfway amused with herself. Once she'd left Maine she'd have to relearn the art of exchanging preliminary conversational pleasantries. In Maine one got directly to the point with a minimum expression of surprise or curiosity.

"Afternoon, Mrs. Patton," Abe Johnson replied with a courtesy that in no way diminished his own dignity. "Mr. James Patton sent Bobby and myself over to give you a hand. Reckon we can take care of things out here."

"*Mr. James Patton*—" Jane blurted out, staring at Abe in surprise as she digested his news. James had instructed his gardener and his grandson to "give her a hand"! Questions whirled through her head. She had to restrain herself from voicing some of them to Abe, who was waiting patiently for her to absorb his announcement and let him and Bobby get about their business.

"That's very good of Mr. Patton to send you and Bobby over to help out." *Why* was James suddenly interested in getting the grounds of Lottie's cottage in shape? Was he the mystery buyer after all? These questions churned inside Jane as she asked casually, "When did you speak to Mr. Patton, Abe?" Perhaps Ted Blockett hadn't gotten in touch with James yet and told him that Lottie Patton had refused to sell.

Abe blinked during the slight pause before he answered. Jane supposed it was his way of displaying surprise at a question that had no relevance to him.

"Five, maybe ten minutes ago." He glanced over to the left in the direction of the adjoining Patton estate.

Jane's pulse quickened as an intuition took hold. "Mr. Patton telephoned you?"

Another blink accompanied by another pause. "No need for a telephone call. Not when he could tell me himself in person."

"In person," Jane echoed, unable to help herself, even though she knew Abe Johnson was finding her reaction most strange. No doubt she was destroying whatever stature she had gained in his eyes from wintering in Maine. It was just coming as a shock to learn that James had come back and was close by. She would go over to his cottage at once and ask him if he was the one who had offered to buy this cottage.

This time James had come by car. A black Ferrari

was parked in front of the cottage. Jane paused beside it a moment, reflecting that the rakish automobile suited its owner, suggesting power and daring.

The front door was open. After only a second's hesitation she entered the cottage without knocking and stood inside the door, listening. She opened her mouth to call out and then closed it when she heard a sound coming from the rear of the house. When had James ever announced his arrival next door?

As she made her way along a hallway and through connecting rooms, Jane was aware of the scent of furniture polish and wax. The cottage was in immaculate condition, much as Lottie's had once been. The occasional muffled sounds led her to the open doorway of a room lined with shelves of books from floor to ceiling and containing dark leather upholstered sofas and easy chairs, with a massive desk at one end. It was obviously a man's room, a combination library and study. James had his back to the door. He was taking selected volumes from the shelves and stacking them on the floor.

Jane stood in the doorway watching him, noting his balanced stance and the fluid play of muscles in his back and arms as he reached up to a high shelf. It was the first time she had ever come upon *him* unawares. Suddenly she wished she had called out or at least had made more noise walking through the house.

"Hello, James."

He froze in reaction to her voice but then visibly relaxed almost instantly. Before wheeling around to face her, he plucked the fat red volume he had been reaching for off the shelf.

"What are you doing?" she asked quickly, uncomfortably aware of his dark scrutiny. Now she wished she had taken the time to change clothes and make herself more presentable.

"Packing." He turned back toward the shelves and continued his task.

"Packing?" Jane took several steps into the room. "What do you mean . . . *packing?"*

James pivoted and brought an armload of books over to those stacked neatly in front of a large wine leather sofa. When he didn't look in her direction, Jane drifted closer. But then he straightened, and as her cautious gaze met his, the currents of awareness coursed between them. Jane was sure that he, too, was remembering their meeting on the lawn just three days ago. Resisting the urge to retreat, she reminded herself of her reason for being there—to ask James if he had offered through a realtor to buy the other Patton cottage. Here in his presence she was more doubtful than ever that he had.

"James, thank you for lending us your gardeners," she began, intending to ask jokingly if he wasn't being a little overeager about getting the grounds of the cottage next door in shape.

James made an abrupt gesture to cut her off and then walked back over to the bookshelves. "Don't mention it. Abe has everything caught up here. He might as well do something to earn his money."

Jane perched on the arm of an easy chair and watched him a moment in silence, feeling the tension flowing from him. She could have pointed out that there was always something for a gardener to occupy his time with on an estate this size. She could have asked him if he employed Bobby full-time too. But it was obvious that James didn't want to discuss his reasons for sending Abe and Bobby over to work on

Lottie's grounds. It also was becoming increasingly obvious that James didn't welcome this visit from her, a situation Jane found intriguing.

"James, why are you taking those books from the cottage?" From where she sat she could read several titles. One of them was *Moby Dick*.

"I'm taking the ones I intend to keep, along with a few items of furniture and some odds and ends I've always liked. The rest will be sold, either with the cottage or separately. I haven't decided yet." While he made this clipped explanation, James pulled books out by twos and threes and then carried the stack over to deposit it by the others.

Jane absorbed the revelation that quite effectively erased any lingering conjecture that James might be the undisclosed buyer Ted Blockett had mentioned. If he were selling this cottage, he certainly wouldn't be trying to buy the one next door just to keep it in the Patton family. And the notion of James harboring any sympathetic feelings toward Lottie and herself was laughable. Why should he?

"If you've no intention of coming here during the summers and using the place, I suppose you may as well sell it," she mused. "Unless you have sentimental reasons for keeping it and passing it on someday to your own heirs." Privately she was thinking that James might just as well have had someone come in and pack up all the books. He seemed to be pulling most of them off the shelves now.

"*Sentimental reasons.*" James's harshly jeering tone made Jane start. She cringed a little as he wheeled around abruptly, but then relaxed a bit when he stood in his tracks, his legs braced apart, his arms loaded with heavy volumes. "How the hell could you expect this place to hold any sentimental attachment for me?" His laugh was unpleasant to her ears. "That would make as much sense as looking back and remembering an abscessed tooth with fond memory. I spent some of the loneliest, most miserable times of my life here." He laughed again, the sound a grating parody of mirth. "Sentimental reasons." The last words were spoken in a quieter tone, more to himself than to her, and they rang with a bitterness that shivered along Jane's spine. There seemed nothing for her to say, especially in light of the fact that she herself must be nothing but a bad memory to James.

And yet she couldn't bring herself to get up and leave, even when it was obvious there was no reason to stay. James certainly didn't want her company. He was moodily absorbed in his selection of books, more deliberate now since his outpouring of bitter emotion.

"You were right a few days ago when you predicted that Aunt Lottie would put up a fight against selling the cottage." In some illogical way Jane was offering him the admission as a kind of compensation for past hostilities. She was frankly miffed when James greeted the news with apparent indifference, continuing his task without comment. Doggedly she continued, relating the scene with the real estate broker the previous day and describing his aunt's behavior toward her since then.

"She thinks I'll give in to her, but I won't," Jane mused in a soft voice laced with steel. By now she felt as though she were talking to herself. James seemed not to be listening. "I'm not saying I'll go so far as to see a lawyer and try to *force* her to sell. I couldn't do that, not after everything she's done for me. But I'm not going to stay here. I'm *not*." Jane suddenly felt

lightheaded with the momentousness of the resolve
she had just worked out for herself. "Well, James,
don't you have anything to say?" It annoyed her that
she had just confided one of the most important
decisions in her life, and he gave no evidence of even
having heard her.

James's fingers closed around a valuable old edition
of *Robinson Crusoe* he'd read every single summer
he'd spent here at the cottage with his grandfather.
For several seconds he didn't dare trust himself to
speak. How could she actually ask in that reproving
tone, *Well, James, don't you have anything to say?* Of
course, he had things to say, lots of things. He
wouldn't be human if he didn't long to remind her that
she could have married *him* six years ago instead of
Terry, whom she'd known at the time wouldn't be
able to support her.

"What's there to say?" Carefully James drew out
the volume of *Robinson Crusoe* and placed it tenderly
on top of the stack of books he balanced against his
body with the other arm. "Certainly you have every
right to think of your own future."

Without so much as a glance toward her, he turned
and carried the books over to the growing mountain
of volumes he had already pulled off the shelves. He'd
have to go through them again, but in the meanwhile
this gave him something to do.

Jane watched him in silence for a full minute and
then got to her feet. "I guess I'd better go and leave
you to your packing," she murmured. It occurred to
her that she was suffering the same lack of welcome at
James's hands that he had met with time after time at
the cottage next door.

James clenched his teeth tightly together to keep

himself from speaking her name and stopping her. All these years he'd been wanting her, and here she was in his house, making overtures. *But why was she here?* Three days ago she had fought him like an angry, spitting cat, the same as always. What had brought on the change?

Jane stopped at the door and turned around slowly, surprised at her own deep reluctance to leave with matters as they were. For the first time in her life, she felt the need to reach out to James, and this was probably the only opportunity she'd ever have.

"I don't suppose you'd want to . . . I mean, later on, you might get tired of working . . . no, I guess you wouldn't," she ended quietly and lifted her shoulders in a resigned shrug. "I can't say that I blame you." Jane turned to leave, feeling as if she'd carried on the whole exchange with herself. In truth, she was as relieved as she was disappointed that James hadn't responded to her fumbling invitation. It was probably better this way.

James couldn't hold back any longer. Swiftly he skirted the barrier of books he'd built up between them and came toward her, stopping when the uncertainty in the honeyed depths of her eyes became mixed with panic.

"If you're suggesting that we see each other later, I think it's an excellent idea," he said softly, his dark eyes challenging hers. "How about dinner at the inn? That is, if you haven't changed your mind. Are you sure you can go through with this, Jane?"

"I don't know what you're talking about," Jane murmured defensively, backing away a half-step. "Dinner at the inn sounds fine." She was having strong second thoughts about making the overture, which James seemed to be interpreting as some kind of proposition, but she couldn't back out without looking like an idiot.

"It's a date then. I'll pick you up, say, about seven-thirty?" James prompted in the same taunting manner, as though he still didn't believe she was serious about going out with him.

"Seven-thirty's fine," Jane concurred hastily, and fled before he could say more or she could change her mind.

As she emerged from the house she shook her head dazedly. It was hard to believe that not only had she agreed to go out with James, of all people, but *she* had asked *him!* He had taken her off guard, giving her that glimpse of him as a lonely, unhappy youth, raising feelings of guilt for her own unfriendliness toward him in the past. For a moment she had seen James as vulnerable and wished that she could make amends.

But then he had changed before her eyes into the old James, hard and aggressive and dangerous, putting her on the defense, where she'd always been with him. Still, she was glad she had made the date. It would be good to have dinner out with a man. It would be fun to dress up a little and get away from the cottage for an evening . . . *get away from Lottie, too.* Jane suffered a pang of guilt for that last thought and walked a little faster.

James watched the empty doorway for long seconds, listening to the quiet sounds of her footsteps. Then he uttered a low curse and lifted one palm up to press it against his forehead. *"The willing fool,"* he murmured aloud, shaking his head and turning back to survey the huge collection of books stacked on the floor. The hell with it! He wasn't going through them again. He'd take them all.

An evening with Jane all to himself. How many years had that been an impossible dream? More than he cared to count. And *she* had asked *him*. Why? The answer was all too obvious. Jane's prospects weren't the best. Widowed, with no money and no job training, she would do well to find herself a wealthy man.

Enter James, right on cue.

It wasn't the kind of scheming logic James could believe Jane capable of on her own. No, in the past three days she'd probably been made to see the light of reason by his dear, despicable aunt. She and Jane both were in for a surprise because James might sample the prize tonight, but he wasn't buying.

Chapter Four

"You look very nice, dear," Lottie said. It was like old times when Jane was getting ready for some social occasion and had to pass Lottie's inspection. Tonight she felt the same flush of pleasure she had felt at sixteen.

And she thought she did look pretty good, under the circumstances. She hadn't been to a hair stylist in years, and her wardrobe consisted almost entirely of what she had owned when Lottie learned that her huge fortune had eroded. The additions since then had been practical clothing. Fortunately, many of her old outfits, like the beige shift she wore tonight, had the timelessness of a classic design and the unmistakable mark of high quality. She had belted it with a gaily printed silk scarf and wore simple pearl studs in her ears and a short string of graduated pearls around her neck. Her hair was swept neatly up into a topknot, and she'd used makeup tonight, finding its application a skill that had grown a little rusty. A touch of eyeshadow and a few strokes of the mascara wand had made her eyes look larger and more luminous. Lip gloss with just a hint of pink emphasized the soft fullness of her mouth. Jane felt feminine and attractive, and she was glad.

When she opened the door to James, the instant appreciation on his face warmed her. He looked attractive enough himself to qualify as an escort for any woman. The lightweight brown tweed jacket had obviously been tailored for no other shoulders but his. The striped silk tie was conservative and correct. His crisp blue Oxford-cloth shirt was the authentic article, all cotton.

It occurred to Jane as she held the door open wide and gestured for James to enter that despite all his wealth, his attire that evening was probably the same vintage as her own!

"Come in and say hello to Aunt Lottie," she prompted him when he stood there, not moving. The expression that darkened his face spoiled her brief illusion that this was a perfectly normal outing.

"James, please." The little lift of her head and the tone of her voice issued a subtle ultimatum.

James stepped across the threshold, annoyed with himself. After all, what was the big deal? It wouldn't kill him to go through the social paces with his aunt. In fact, there might be some satisfaction in showing her she no longer had the power to affect him at all.

"James, how *nice* to see you!" Lottie Patton's gushing tones matched the expression on her face. James had to exert all his self-control to keep from drawing back when his aunt rose from the sofa and came toward him with both hands extended. He couldn't remember when she had ever touched him in the past. As he inclined his head in a polite little gesture and took her hands very briefly in his, he had to fight down the bile rising in his throat.

"It's nice to see you again, too, Aunt Lottie." He took some pleasure in making the words sound mechanical and empty, but yet totally free of the old irony.

The scene was painful for Jane to observe. The motive behind Lottie's unprecedented friendliness would be transparent to James. No doubt he would be gloating behind that impassive exterior. And yet, surprisingly, Jane couldn't detect even a hint of contempt in James's voice as he dutifully answered his aunt's routine inquiries. At the earliest opportunity Jane stepped in and suggested that James probably had a reservation for dinner.

To James it seemed like a rehearsed cue that his aunt seized upon, bidding them to be on their way and have a delightful evening. The coy expression in her blue eyes curdled his blood. It had been bad enough realizing that Jane was desperate enough to give herself to him, but to think of her in league with his aunt was more than he could tolerate.

"Apparently absence does make the heart grow fonder," he commented sarcastically when he and Jane were seated in the Ferrari. He twisted the key and took pleasure in the response of the powerful engine.

Jane bit her lip, struggling between the old demands of loyalty and an urge to be honest with him. In the end she couldn't bring herself to speak openly of her mother-in-law's groveling manner. James was shrewd enough to see behind it without any commentary from Jane and know that his aunt was trying to mend the old breach in the hope that he would be generous toward her. Jane found it impossible, though, not to resent Lottie for having cast a pall over the evening before it even began.

They were dining at the Islesboro Inn, like the two Patton cottages located on the southern end of the island and just minutes away. The original establishment of that name, built in 1890, had known an illustrious history in its heyday but had fallen upon hard times and finally been torn down in the fifties. The present Islesboro Inn was a former private summer cottage of roughly the same vintage as the Patton cottages. Converted into a luxury hotel, it catered to moneyed guests seeking a quiet holiday in an old-world atmosphere. Its dining room offered excellent Continental cuisine, and the awning-shaded terrace was a favorite gathering place for cocktails among the wealthier summer residents.

"I guess this wasn't such a good idea," Jane commented when she and James were seated at a table on the terrace and awaiting the drinks they had ordered, a daiquiri for Jane and a Beefeater martini on the rocks for James. It was promising to be a wretched evening, with James tense and moody and herself mentally picking her way through conversational offerings and feeling as though she were in a danger zone mined with explosives.

"No," he agreed tersely, and then visibly willed himself to relax.

"I've been trying to think of something 'safe' we could talk about." She lifted her shoulders in a little shrug to indicate her lack of success so far and then

waited while the cocktails were served. When James
lifted his martini to his lips and took a healthy slug,
she sipped at her daiquiri.

"What was it like for you—living here the year
round the last six years?" he asked, putting his glass
down with a little thud.

Jane lifted her brows delicately. *A "safe" topic?*
After the initial instinctive resistance, she discovered
to her surprise that she *wanted* to answer him. She
wanted to talk about the last six years.

"What was it like . . ." She sipped her daiquiri and
then smiled as an amusing analogy offered itself.
"Kind of like a reverse Cinderella story, in a way.
Starting off at the ball and ending up cleaning out the
ashes in the fireplace—" She broke off at the cynical
light gleaming in his eyes, able to guess his thoughts.
There had been a wicked stepmother in the Cinderella
fable and a fairy godmother. Which was Lottie?
Before he could say anything that would require her
to go on the defensive, Jane made a self-disparaging
sound.

"Don't I sound like a self-pitying soul! First, there
was the tremendous mental adjustment that had to be
made. After having so much for so long, it wasn't easy
to accept the fact that there was no longer the money
for servants, travel, clothes, jewelry . . . all the *things*
that I was used to having for the asking." She waited
a moment as James picked up his glass and took a
large swallow. Only then did it flash into her mind
what he might be thinking: She would still have had
all those accustomed luxuries if she had married
him.

"At first I wondered what in the world I would do
with all the time. I was so used to going and doing

and . . . spending." She smiled. "I soon learned how much effort is involved in just the simple routine of living. There was food to be bought at the market, meals to be prepared, and then the cleaning up afterward. Clothes had to be laundered and mended, linen changed on the beds, fires built in the fireplaces. It all sounds so simple—but I didn't know how to do any of it!"

"And I don't suppose my aunt helped you with any of that," James put in, unable to keep out the tinge of sarcasm he knew would affront her.

Jane stiffened involuntarily at his tone but bit back an automatic retort. She didn't want to spend the evening fighting with him over Lottie.

"No, she didn't. That was my fault more than hers. I didn't allow her to do anything." She ignored the skeptical twist of his lips. "At first the day-to-day chores used up most of my time, until I got better at them. Then there was time left over . . . to read, to do needlework, to think, to look at and listen to the world around me in all its different moods and seasons." Jane looked across the terraced lawn of the inn with its immaculately tended flowerbeds and gazed at the bay, thinking of how she had contemplated it in a thousand different lights. "And, of course, I wasn't alone," she continued softly. "There was Terry and Aunt Lottie to share things with, good *and* bad."

James felt a twisting in his guts that he recognized as jealousy. *And now that Terry was gone, she wanted more than the spartan life she had lived with him.* That was why she was here with James tonight.

"So that's what it was like for me the last six years." Jane had brought her gaze back to James. Her tone was brisk, indicating that she had said enough on the subject.

"And now you're ready for a change."

Jane was genuinely puzzled by his flat tone and the hard expression on his face.

"Yes, I am. What's wrong with that?"

He shrugged. "Nothing's wrong with it. Excuse me while I check on our table."

Over dinner Jane did her best to keep the conversation away from talk of herself, but somehow James kept working in questions, so that by the time they had finished the dessert course, she realized she had revealed a great deal more about her life on Islesboro the past six years. She had even told him what her needlework had come to mean to her, more than just a pastime but a vital creative outlet. Not once, though, had he mentioned Terry's name.

"We've talked of almost nothing but me," Jane protested lightly when they had left the dining room and gone back out on the terrace for a liqueur. "Tell me what you've been doing all these years."

"Basically I'm a businessman," James replied matter-of-factly. "I try to keep abreast of the stock market and look after my investments. I take an active interest in several companies in which I'm a major stockholder, one in particular which manufactures computer software."

"Do you live in Boston?" Jane was remembering his grandfather's somber brick mansion.

"No, New York. I have an apartment there." Actually he owned the whole building. "Once or twice I've been tempted to buy a getaway place somewhere, like St. Croix, but I don't like the idea of going back to the same place over and over. I'd rather rent a villa or charter a yacht." James heard the undertone of restlessness in his own voice and knew he could have added that in spite of all the material ties that connected him to his ancestry, he was a strangely rootless man.

"What about your grandfather's house in Boston? And his Palm Beach house? Did you sell them?" She sounded faintly skeptical because it wouldn't make sense that he had sold the other places and kept the Islesboro cottage this long.

James lifted his eyebrows as he raised his snifter of brandy to his lips. He held the fiery smoothness of the liquor in his mouth, savoring it before he answered.

"I couldn't sell them since they never belonged to me."

Jane stared at him disbelievingly. "You don't mean your grandfather sold them before he died?"

"No, he didn't sell them." The lighting on the terrace was dim, but Jane saw comprehension cross James's features. He nodded slowly and took another sip of brandy. "You think I inherited everything from my grandfather."

Her eyes probed his countenance. "Well, didn't you? Terry didn't get a cent." She made no effort to conceal her view that an injustice had been done.

"I am aware of that fact. Neither did I. My grandfather left his entire fortune to a foundation that he established to support nautical museums and retirement homes for seafaring men."

Jane couldn't believe her ears. She had spent the last three years believing James had inherited his grandfather's entire estate. "You inherited *nothing?*" she persisted. "But didn't you even contest the will?"

James's eyes narrowed. He knew the channels her

thoughts were taking. "Why should I?" he queried softly. "My grandfather was in his right mind. I didn't need or want his money. After all, hadn't he done enough for me?" The last words were ironic but not bitter. He'd decided long ago that his grandfather had done the best of which he was capable. Besides, the old man was dead now.

"No, *you* didn't need his money!" Jane burst out and then checked herself, biting down hard on her bottom lip. It galled her to think that Terry's grandfather had given all his money away to strangers when one of his two grandsons was living in virtual poverty. And James, damn him, could have done something to rectify the wrong!

Her charged anger sparked an old amalgam of emotions that James had tried for years to rid himself of. Tonight, though, he would *not* let it master him. He reached across the table, took the stemmed glass from her rigid grasp, and moved it aside. Then he captured her hands loosely in his, feeling her pulse in the slender fingers.

"Jane, did you really think that I, of all people, should go to bat for my dear cousin Terry?" he chided her softly. "Why would I? In God's name, *why*, when he'd always gotten every single thing that I could have wanted? Even when he couldn't hope to support a wife on his own, he had *you*."

Jane tried to pull her hands away, but James tightened his grasp and held them. She could feel the tensile strength in his fingers and felt her old sense of helplessness in the face of his brute superiority. No one occupied the tables nearest them, but they still were not alone on the terrace, and Jane didn't want to make a public scene.

"It still galls you that you lost out to Terry when I married him instead of you, doesn't it, James?" she whispered fiercely. "You always had to lord it over Terry, who couldn't hope to compete with you in any sport. He was never involved in any contest with you over me! He cared about me for myself, not as some kind of prize or trophy!"

James let go of her hands abruptly and drew back in his chair, struggling to subdue the aggression she had unleashed in him. She was at least partly right. It made him sick inside to think of Jane married to Terry, sleeping with him, granting him all the sweet intimacies of her body. James had wanted all of that for himself. But had he wanted her only to keep his cousin from having her? He quite honestly didn't know.

"I'm sorry," Jane murmured with her head turned to one side. "I really had hoped . . ." What had she hoped? She didn't really know, but certainly she hadn't wanted to spend the evening resurrecting old hostilities.

James knew damned well what she had hoped: to hide her true feelings toward him, which apparently hadn't changed much. He'd been vacillating all evening, one part of him urging *Take her!* but coming up against a deep reservation. Now the cynical opportunist took command.

"How about a walk?" he proposed, getting up.

Jane hesitated only because the suggestion had taken her by surprise. "A walk? Okay." Anything would be better than sitting here battering at each other.

They descended cement steps, taking them down several levels of the terraced rear grounds, and wandered off at a right angle toward the bay, soon beyond the view of the inn guests lingering on the terrace. Jane felt his hand come to rest lightly on the small of her back, and she shivered.

"Cold?" The palm of his hand slid up her back and his arm circled her shoulders.

"No." Actually she had been conscious of the cool night air, but suddenly she was flooded with warmth as his steps slowed and the arm around her shoulders impeded her own forward movement. They stopped underneath a large pine tree, and James stepped in front of her, both arms sliding around her in a loose embrace that left a small distance between them.

"James . . ." She looked up at him, but it was very dark in the shadow of the tree. Even without seeing his expression, though, she could sense a difference between this time and all the others when James had taken her into his arms. There would be no force.

"Yes, Jane?" His hands moved lightly down to her hips and then upward to shape their curve and clasp her waist. Jane felt herself leaning slightly toward him, and her feet took the tiny half step necessary to correct her balance and bring her closer to him. Her arms felt awkward hanging down. She brought her hands up and rested them on his shoulders. The suspense of the moment was making her heart thump hard in her breast.

"James . . ." she said again, and her hands slid tentatively inward along his shoulders toward his neck.

The unspoken capitulation had an instant and powerful effect upon James. His body hardened with a raging eagerness to possess her, but he exerted a monumental control, bending down to brush his lips teasingly against hers and then take lingering tastes at each corner. Her lips softened and clung to his. He could feel her breath coming in little gusts.

It was exquisite agony not to reach down for her buttocks and crush her hard against the swelling ache of his groin, but he managed somehow not to. While he tasted the curves of her lower lip with his tongue, he caressed her back and shoulders and then slid his hands around to the front of her waist and up to her breasts. The soft moan escaping her lips was a signal to squeeze the rounded fullness and pinch the hardened peaks he could feel through the layers of cloth.

Jane closed her arms tight around his neck and clung to him, the need washing through her. What he was doing to her body felt too wonderful for words. It had *always* been so. Her hands clasped the back of his head and she kissed him hungrily, opening her mouth to his tongue and yielding voluntarily what he had only gained by plundering in the past.

When she had lost her breath and had to tip back her head to take in oxygen, his hands ceased the heavenly caresses to her breasts and slid down to her bottom, lifting her and bringing her body hard against his. Her soft moan coincided with the groan that tore out of his throat as their bodies made the intimate but incomplete contact.

Even in her aroused state Jane knew a moment's embarrassment for her quick abandon. "It's been such a long time . . ." she murmured, and knew almost instantly she had spoken the wrong words when she felt his infinitesimal withdrawal.

James slowly lowered her so that her feet touched

the ground. His hands slid up to her waist and he eased her a little distance away.

"James, you *knew* I wasn't a virgin!" she protested, knowing all the while that wasn't the issue.

James stood her back farther away from him and then took his hands from her waist. "Virgin or not, a bed of pine needles is not my idea of the ideal place to make love." In a strange way he was almost grateful to her for restoring him to his sanity with that reminder that she had given Terry first claim to her body. For a minute there James had been lost in the mindless ecstasy of her unforced response to him. He had lost all awareness of the past or the future. He hadn't been taking her; he'd been giving himself.

"James, I really cannot believe how . . . how perverse you are!" Jane still felt weak with the passion he had aroused in her and vaguely wronged as she realized he had no intention of going further, on this bed of pine straw or anywhere else. "All these years you've been accosting me against my will, and the moment I respond, you're not interested!"

"Oh, but I am definitely still interested, Jane," he contradicted her, knowing all too well he spoke the truth. "It's just that old competitive spirit of mine that you keep bringing up. I can't help wondering how I compare to Terry in the lovemaking department." There was an element of truth in that, along with the calculated intent to antagonize her and put distance between them.

Jane sucked in her breath. "You're lying, James. You've never doubted for a second that you were better than Terry at anything you tried to do. I'm surprised you didn't take up painting."

Her anger was an aphrodisiac. God, he still wanted

her. The scent of her was in his nostrils. The feel of her lingered on his hands and lips.

"You still haven't answered my question. Did my cousin turn you on the way I do?" he taunted half-heartedly.

For a brief moment Jane almost told him the truth. After all, what harm would it do Terry? But in the end, loyalty won out. "Terry was a wonderful lover," she told him. Terry had been tender and sweet, and there had been a time or two approaching rapture, but never in her husband's arms had she known the wild pleasure that James could set off with just the stroke of his hand.

"That probably accounts for your contentment playing nurse and housemaid while he was alive." The tinge of sarcasm didn't come close to reflecting the surge of jealousy that had seized him at her less-than-convincing declaration of her deceased husband's sexual prowess. The truth or falsity of her claim had little importance. It was that untainted loyalty, that singleminded devotion to those Jane favored with her love that James envied his dead cousin.

"I suppose you may as well take me home," Jane suggested with a dispirited little sigh. It had been a horribly disappointing evening, starting out and ending badly. Only briefly, somewhere in the middle, had she felt she was getting to know the James she had just glimpsed that afternoon in the library of his cottage, the man who had openly admitted vulnerability when he spoke with revealing bitterness about his unhappy and lonely youth.

"I suppose so," James agreed readily. As they retraced their steps back to the inn, he carefully refrained from touching her, not even trusting himself to take her arm or guide her with a light pressure of his hand at the small of her back. That had been a close call there under the pine tree. It had awakened such intense longing that James was shaken to the core. He had only been fooling himself to think that he could take whatever sexual favors Jane offered and walk away, safe. Whatever it was that he had wanted and been denied for so many years eluded his understanding, but the whole complex tangle of emotions somehow involved Jane. He didn't want to possess just her body—he wanted *her*, all of her.

Neither of them spoke until they were seated in the Ferrari and James was in the process of fitting the key into the ignition.

"Why have you kept the cottage this long?" Jane asked unexpectedly.

James finished inserting the key, but sat back without starting the engine. Several answers, all with some element of truth, came easily to mind. He sorted through them aloud. "Oh, I don't know exactly why. Maybe I never really felt a sense of ownership. The cottage always seemed more like my grandfather's than mine. As you know, he came up here each summer until three years ago." He drummed his fingers on the wheel with its leather sheathing. "And, too, both the cottages were built by my great-grandfather and have always been in the Patton family. Say whatever you like, it's not easy to break with tradition." He shrugged impatiently and started the engine. "Hell, I don't know why I haven't gotten rid of the place. Maybe it was easier not to."

Jane appreciated the honesty of his reply and chose not to delve any deeper, even though she would have liked to. "It's interesting that you do feel the pressures of Patton family tradition," she mused as they pulled out onto the highway. "I didn't know if you would. In the back of her mind I think Aunt Lottie has always believed that if worse came to worst, you would step in and prevent her from losing the cottage." Jane paused, assuming that he, too, was remembering his aunt's reception of him earlier that evening, which had been motivated by the unfounded —and doubtlessly futile—hope Jane had mentioned.

Minutes passed, and it seemed that James would drive her home in total silence until he asked tersely, "What about you, Jane? Did you think that too? Did you think I'd come to the rescue?" James knew he was driving too fast along the curving, two-lane highway, but he felt completely in control of the powerful automobile, and he needed the speed.

Jane thought for a moment before she answered, one part of her enjoying the sensation of speed and power. "Yes, I think that perhaps I *did* think you would 'come to the rescue,' James," she mused, and then waited while he braked and turned into the entrance of the lane. The powerful beams opened up the lane like a great plow turning a furrow. "You know, I wasn't even aware that deep down I thought that. Now I know you won't." There was a simple finality in the last statement and a total absence of reproach or resentment.

"What 'form' did you expect this 'rescue' to take?" James inquired tersely, despite his firm intentions to maintain silence. As if he didn't already know.

Jane glanced over at him in surprise. "What 'form?' Why, money, of course. What else?" She forced an ironic little laugh. "You must know that people without money always assume that those who have a lot can spare some and never miss it." In a way it was embarrassing but also a relief to speak so openly.

"I see," James said stiffly, bringing the car to a halt. He'd wanted her to put it into words, but she'd denied him that. If she had come right out and admitted the truth, if she had said, *James, I was hoping you'd marry me,* God help him, he didn't know that he wouldn't have taken her up on it.

Jane opened her door, swung one foot down to the ground, and then turned toward him, taking in the erect posture and stony profile. He was obviously waiting impatiently for her to get out of the car, out of his life—forever.

"Good night, James. Thank you for the dinner. It's too late, I know, but I really am . . . sorry." Jane wasn't clear on exactly what she was sorry about, but her regret was deep and genuine.

James kept a hard grip on the wheel. "Good-bye, Jane. It's been nice. Old times and all that." The harsh undertone was strikingly inappropriate for the words.

Dissatisfaction washed through Jane as she got out of the car and closed the door. Before she had reached the front door of the cottage, James was already gone. There was just the red wink of the taillights through the trees and then darkness as he drove out of her life with no intention of ever returning. He had said "good-bye," not "good night."

Chapter Five

Jane was surprised when she pulled down the flap of the mailbox and saw the letter postmarked Jacksonville, Florida, the address written in her mother's neat handwriting. After all these years, it was still strange to see the return address headed by Mrs. Thomas Duggans.

There was no other mail in the box. Jane tore open the envelope, intending to read the letter right there. Correspondence between herself and her mother consisted primarily of cards at birthdays and major holidays with a scrawled note. It was definitely something of a surprise to receive a letter.

She hadn't gotten past "Dear Jane" when she heard the engine of the Ferrari and looked around to see the low-slung black automobile come into sight. James was driving fast. He obviously had no intention of turning into her lane. Jane barely had time to wonder if he would just whiz on past, when James stepped on the brakes and brought the car smartly to a halt.

"Hello. You're going somewhere in a hurry," she greeted him conversationally, aware of his inspection that took in her tailored navy slacks and plaid blouse. For the past two days she had taken more care with her appearance.

"I always get in a hurry when I start out somewhere to gorge myself on fresh lobster," he countered. His bags were packed and in the trunk. He planned to take the ferry over to the mainland, have lunch, and then head for New York. "How about you? Got a taste for lobster?"

"I always have a taste for lobster." The idea of climbing into the Ferrari and setting off on the spur of the moment had a powerful appeal that made Jane feel more like sixteen than twenty-six. "Is that an invitation?"

"Hop in."

James watched her hesitate. When she glanced behind her in the direction of the bay, and then back to him, he shook his head, already sorry now that he had given in to impulse. "You're a big girl now. You don't have to have my aunt's permission." He revved the powerful engine.

"Of course I don't, but she might worry." He hadn't understood the nature of her indecision, and she chose not to explain. More than likely Lottie would go all day without eating if Jane weren't there to prepare something for her. Well, it wouldn't hurt her to look after herself for once. After all, she needed to know what it was going to be like if she did insist upon staying on in Islesboro without Jane, for

Jane was more determined with every passing day that she was going elsewhere to pick up her life.

"I can call her from the restaurant."

James watched her as she walked around the front of the car and thought fleetingly of chance. Why had she been standing there beside the road? Now he'd have to take the ferry back over here. He couldn't blame chance for making him issue the invitation, though, could he? It had popped out without any premeditation.

"This is fun!" Jane's smile reflected her sense of adventure as she slid into the low bucket seat beside him and clipped her seat belt together. As the car surged forward she relaxed into the deep leather cushions. "Have I mentioned that I love your car?"

James glanced over at her, taking in the unaffected enthusiasm on her face. "It's a great car," he agreed, and lessened his pressure on the accelerator. "A little hard to restrain though," he added with a wry grin.

The atmosphere between them was easy on the brief drive to Grindle's Point, where roughly a dozen vehicles were already lined up and waiting for the arrival of the ferry. James pulled up behind the last one and turned off the key. Over to their right was the Grindle Point lighthouse, maintained as a museum now along with the attached lightkeeper's house. A visitor to Islesboro would declare the old lighthouse quaint and different, square rather than round, but Jane had seen it too many times to even consciously notice it.

"Mind if I read my letter?" she inquired, pulling it once again out of the envelope.

"Of course not."

Jane scanned the letter quickly and then read it

through again, more out of a sense of conscience than
anything else. "From my mother," she told James,
refolding the letter and slipping it back into the
envelope. He glanced around at her, his interest
awakened at her tone. "She lives in Jacksonville,
Florida, with her husband—I never have been able to
think of him as my stepfather." There was the same
rueful note, almost apologetic.

"Your mother. Frankly I'd forgotten all about her."
James was searching his memory for a clear picture
and finding only a hazy one. "That's right. She
married a workingman, didn't she, and incurred my
aunt's wrath?"

"A plumber. My mother met him at Aunt Lottie's
house in Boston. It was when Aunt Lottie was having
the old carriage house turned into a guest house. He
was a widower with three children. He and my mother
lived in Boston only a year after they were married.
Then they moved down to Florida."

"How old were you then—fifteen or sixteen?"

"Sixteen. I was in school in Switzerland." She had
been living in a world entirely foreign to the one her
mother had chosen. "I met my mother's husband and
her new stepchildren that summer when I came home,
and after she moved to Florida I visited her several
times. But it was always so awkward for her and for
me. Her husband carried a chip on his shoulder
because of Aunt Lottie's attitude that my mother had
married 'beneath' her. The fact that I stayed with
Aunt Lottie seemed proof to him that I felt the same
way."

"Did your mother try to get you to live with her?"

"No, she didn't." Jane's voice was full of remem-
brance. "The situation made it impossible for her to

speak her mind openly, but I was able to understand that she wanted what was best for me. Looking back, I think it was a testimony of my mother's love that she gave me over to Aunt Lottie."

James was glad the ferry had docked. He knew Jane wouldn't appreciate hearing his thoughts on the wisdom of her mother's sacrifice.

"Have you considered going down to live with your mother when you leave Islesboro?" He asked this question after they had driven aboard the ferry and had gotten out of the car to stand by the railing. Jane had to adjust her thoughts since the subject of her mother had seemed to be dropped. She shook her head.

"It wouldn't be fair to her. I know she'd tell me to come if I asked her, but she has her hands full, not to mention her house. Her husband's youngest child, a boy, is still in high school. And then there's a divorced daughter with two children living at home, a baby and a two-year-old. Her husband deserted her. My mother baby-sits with the children while their mother works during the day. No, I can't go and live with my mother. . . ."

James knew there was more involved than just a crowded house. Jane had made her choice between her real and her surrogate mother years ago. The ties that bound her to his aunt were powerful. He didn't think for a minute that Jane was going to leave her behind in Islesboro, not to go to her mother or anywhere else.

They drove north to Belfast and lunched at a small restaurant right on the harbor. Jane discovered that James had not been joking when he said he planned to "gorge" on lobster.

"But I can eat only one lobster!" she protested when he gave his order, *four* lobsters for the two of them.

"Better too much than not enough," he replied, unswayed. "What we don't eat you can always take home with you." He settled back in the plain wooden chair and took a gulp of draft beer from an icy goblet.

"How are you coming along at the cottage?" she asked him, taking a sip of her own beer. She hadn't seen him during the past two days following their dinner at the Islesboro Inn.

"I'm all finished." James thought of the luggage in the trunk of his car.

"Oh. Then you'll be leaving?"

"I'll be leaving," he agreed and raised the goblet to his lips again. "What about you?"

It took a moment for her to comprehend. Her face clouded over as she thought of her several attempts the past two days to reason with her mother-in-law about selling the cottage and moving off Islesboro.

"Aunt Lottie won't even *talk* about selling the cottage." Jane sighed her exasperation. "I don't think she really believes I'll leave without her."

James didn't either. "Why don't you set a definite date?"

Jane thought about the suggestion. At first it caused a little nervous sensation in the pit of her stomach, but she knew he was right. "The end of August. That's as long as I'll stay." The nervousness was even stronger with that statement, but it was blended with excitement now.

The lobsters were brought to the table steaming hot, along with bowls of drawn butter. She set to work on her lobster, her mind racing. Since Lottie didn't drive and certainly couldn't afford a chauffeur, Jane would take the old Lincoln. As Terry's widow surely she was entitled to something.

Jane didn't have much money, but some instinct had led her to keep her earnings from the co-op separate this spring. She would continue to save the proceeds from sale of her needlework throughout the rest of the summer. By the end of August she should have a little nest egg, enough to pay rent and buy food while she got a job to support herself.

James was too busy eating to take note of her absorbed silence, or if he did notice it, he apparently assumed that, like himself, she was concentrating totally upon the enjoyment of the succulent food. When he had disposed of two of the lobsters, he heaved a satisfied sigh and sat back, surveying the carnage.

"Ah, bliss," he pronounced, and wiped his hands with a wet napkin before signaling the waitress for another draft beer.

Jane dragged her thoughts back to the present. "Don't you have lobster in New York?"

"Yes, but it never tastes as good as it does here in Maine. These fellows probably haven't been out of the bay more than a few hours."

Jane grimaced, pushing her tray back and reaching for her own wet napkin. "I wish you wouldn't speak of them so personally. It makes me feel like a cannibal."

James grinned. "That was to make you lose your appetite. Don't you want your other lobster?"

"*James!* You're not really going to eat another one?" She eyed him in disbelief.

"Yep." He took his fresh draft beer directly from the waitress's hand and downed a good third of it before he set to work on the remaining lobster. Jane watched him, shaking her head every now and then. He looked like anything but the heir to a vast fortune.

"James," she said idly, struck by a sudden curiosity. "What did you keep out of the cottage?"

He cracked a claw and broke it apart. "Books. A few paintings. The rug in the dining room. A couple of old chests." Not enough to require two days of deliberation, Jane was thinking when he paused to take a deep swallow of beer. "Some knickknacks I thought Old Nan might get a kick out of having."

"Old Nan? Who's she?"

James took his time about answering. He cleaned his hands thoroughly, picked up the tray of debris in front of him, and put it over to one side.

"She was my nurse from the time I was born. When my parents were killed and I went to live with my grandfather, she came with me. I'm not sure how old she is, but she must be pushing eighty. She lives in Florida, near St. Petersburg, in one of those retirement communities where the old people have their own bungalow but there's a central complex with a dining room, an infirmary, and recreational facilities."

"It sounds very nice." *And expensive.* Jane didn't have to ask who was footing the bill.

"Yes, it is. Old Nan deserves it," he returned evenly. James had caught the faint reproach in her voice and understood it at once. He had seen to the security and comfort of an old servant while he ignored the plight of his own kin. There was good reason. His aunt hadn't even made him welcome in her house. Old Nan had loved him. As for Jane, he'd offered to take care of her, and she had refused him.

The brief exchange, though it had been largely unspoken, nonetheless disrupted the companionable atmosphere between them. They found themselves on opposite sides of a line that had been drawn long ago and yet apparently was ineradicable, even with time and much changed circumstances.

There was little conversation on the return drive. James intended to get her back to Islesboro and then be on his way. But when he got close to Lincoln Beach and the ferry landing, he found himself not slowing up. Jane glanced over at him inquiringly.

"You in a hurry to get back?" he asked casually, his eyes on the road.

"No."

He turned his head then and let his gaze intersect with hers. "Good."

The abbreviated exchange cleared the air of tension and established a kind of truce based upon what had not been said. For whatever reason, and neither of them was saying why, they didn't want the time together to end. The next few hours were a strange kind of procrastination as they wandered through what was familiar but neutral territory, since it was not mined with memories as was Islesboro. Both of them sensed the importance of postponing the return to the island.

In Camden, James pulled into the parking lot at the harbor. When they had gotten out of the car he reached for her hand and she gave it to him. He laced his fingers in hers as they strolled along the busy dock. It was Saturday, and the Windjammer fleet was in, adding to the flurry of activity in the harbor. Crew members on the historic old schooners, now employed in the charter trade, were busy washing down decks,

repairing equipment, and loading supplies and firewood for the wood-burning cookstoves. On shore,
people of all ages sat on the benches, watching the
harbor activity and basking in the sunshine. Children
milled around, eating ice cream cones.

Jane saw it all through a haze. The sun beat down
warmly upon her head, but she wasn't even aware of it
as a possible source of the heat in her body. That
came directly from the clasp of James's hand. The
intimacy between them grew like a palpable thing, fed
by the pulse of his flesh, the expression in his eyes, the
tone of his voice and hers as they made desultory,
meaningless conversation that had nothing to do with
the real topic: the intense awareness between them.

When they had walked along for a while and then
gotten back into the car again, James drove south,
retreating farther away from the ferry landing at
Lincoln Beach. Jane made no comment, asked no
questions. At Rockport, he parked at the picturesque
little harbor that, like the one at Camden, was popular with both townspeople and visitors alike on such a
fine June weekend.

They held hands once again as they strolled through
the park area, paused by the sculpture of a seal whose
plaque explained the subject as André, Rockport's
"most famous citizen," and then walked over to the
opposite side of the harbor, where a crowd had
gathered to watch André perform, as he did each
afternoon in the summer.

James stood next to her, his arm lightly around her
shoulders, but then as more people gathered and
pressed closer, he dropped back behind her, his arms
sliding lightly around her waist. Jane fixed her gaze on
the partly submerged cage out in the harbor that was

André's summer home. She wasn't really seeing the gray speckled seal as he tossed a ball through a basketball hoop and then caught the ball on his nose. She didn't even feel any pain when several children straining to get free of their parents trampled on her feet. James had pulled her back against him. His knuckles were rising and rubbing the undercurves of her breasts. As she leaned back, giving him her weight, she felt the heat of his breath at her neck and then his murmured words, "Jane, I want you."

She turned around, not caring who saw her or even who heard, and looked up into his eyes, seeing the desire there. "I want you too, James," she whispered back. Their eyes held, exchanging a primal message of need. She could tell from the rise and fall of his chest that his heart was beating fast too.

"Let's go." He led her through the crowd, opening up the way.

The brief sensual interlude had been totally spontaneous on both sides. On the walk back to the car and then on the return drive, they both were seized by an awkwardness that neither of them made an effort to dispel. Jane wondered why James didn't touch her now as he had been doing, why he didn't defuse the situation with some joking remark. The fact that he did neither kept her tense and silent in her seat until, finally, when the ferry touched shore on the Islesboro side, she couldn't tolerate the unnatural atmosphere a moment longer.

"James—" she began on a note of uncertainty.

"Changed your mind?" His foot pressed down on the Ferrari as he turned onto the highway. The car shot ahead.

Jane was jerked forward so that if she hadn't been

wearing her seat belt, she would have had to brace herself to keep from being flung into the windshield.

"No, I haven't 'changed my mind,'" she snapped, irritated now as well as baffled by the way he was acting. "I never made it up in the first place!" She hesitated. "James, my 'mind' had nothing to do with . . . with what I said to you in Rockport. It was just something I felt at the time—have you changed *your* mind?"

He glanced over at her and then fixed his gaze back on the road, his lips twisted into a mirthless little smile.

"A thousand times."

Jane watched his profile intently, expecting him to explain the cryptic statement. When it became apparent that he didn't intend to, she lost all patience.

"James, I think you'd better just take me home," she ordered crisply, and then fastened her attention on the road, determined that she wouldn't say another word until he did. The frustration and hurt welled inside her. Why had he said that to her in Rockport and then immediately proceeded to give her the cold shoulder? It just didn't make any sense. From the looks of things, he obviously intended to make no explanations. When the Ferrari slowed in preparation for turning into her lane, Jane had suddenly had more than enough of James's inexplicable behavior.

"You can just let me out here," she blurted angrily.

James hit the brake, and the powerful automobile came to a jarring halt, but before she could open the door, he reached across to the handle, imprisoning her in the seat with the length of his arm.

Jane briefly considered trying to jerk the door open and spring free, but then she dismissed the impulse, knowing that the attempt would be futile. Instead, she pushed herself back against her seat and eyed him warily.

"Well?" she challenged him.

James held her gaze a long moment and shook his head slightly at what he was able to read in the golden depths. She expected her resistance to provoke a sexual assault, as it always had before. "Uh-uh, sweetheart. Never again like that. I don't intend to make it easy for you anymore."

Jane sucked her breath in harder as James leaned closer, taking his hand from the car door and bringing it in a leisurely fashion to her chest, where he brushed his fingertips lightly across the peaks of her breasts, his eyes holding hers captive. What he saw in them plainly pleased him, but it aroused him too. His voice was husky with suppressed passion when he spoke.

"I'll be over at my cottage, waiting for you."

He settled back into his seat again, facing forward. That was clearly all he intended to say. There was still no explanation of the way he had been acting. More confused than ever, Jane swung open the door and climbed out. She didn't know which one of the conflicting messages on James's face and in his voice to heed: *Please come. Don't come.*

"I'll be there after supper, James," she announced firmly and slammed the door. The car leaped away like a low-crouching black panther. Jane looked after it, already regretting the commitment but knowing she would have gone anyway. Deep inside she felt the same combination of yearning and dread that she had read on James's face. It seemed that neither of them really wanted or could prevent what would happen between them tonight. The two of them had been moving toward this moment in their lives as inevitably as two cosmic bodies destined to collide. The metaphor was anything but a comfortable one, and yet it fit Jane's present perception of her relationship with James.

Lottie had managed quite well in Jane's absence, even to preparing her own lunch, and was in a cheerful mood, pleased that Jane had spent much of the day with James and would see him again that evening. Jane wished that she could somehow convince the older woman that no help would be forthcoming from James. He had no intention of providing for his aunt, and whatever happened between him and Jane, tonight or any other night, wasn't likely to change his attitude or have any effect upon Jane's or Lottie's future. Eventually Lottie would be forced to come to that conclusion on her own. In the meanwhile, Jane couldn't give up trying to make her mother-in-law see reality.

"James has finished picking out the things he intends to keep from his cottage. He'll be leaving soon and won't be coming back, I expect. He asked when I'd be leaving, and I told him the end of August." Jane's plans seemed even more real to her now that she had spoken them aloud twice, to James and now to Lottie. She braced herself for a reaction that wasn't forthcoming.

"And what did James say to that?" Lottie put in with transparent eagerness, as though Jane's answer to James had been the most clever kind of subterfuge.

"He didn't say anything—what *should* he say? Aunt Lottie, James couldn't care less what either one of us does! He has nothing but bad memories of his summers here on Islesboro, nothing but bad memories of you and me . . . and Terry. James is going to leave in the next few days—maybe tomorrow—and that's the last we'll probably ever see of him!" Mixed in with Jane's vehemence was a note of regret that she hadn't intended to be there. It undermined Jane's purpose of making Lottie come to grips with James's indifference to their plight.

The care that Jane took with her appearance that evening did not escape Lottie's notice or dampen her hopes of a serious relationship between her wealthy nephew and her daughter-in-law. *What Lottie doesn't know,* Jane told herself a bit defensively, *is that James has reawakened the woman in me. I've simply begun to remember how nice it is to dress up and feel attractive in the eyes of a man. That's all.*

James was expecting her. He had changed into dark slacks and a burgundy shirt left open at the neck. As soon as Jane pulled up in front of the cottage in the old Lincoln, he was there at the front door, waiting for her. She thought at first he would take her right into his arms. She could feel the sheer sexuality of his gaze as it swept over her, taking in the softly feminine blue dress with its gathered skirt and graceful long sleeves.

He led her into the living room, where he had a fire burning in the fireplace and a bottle of wine chilling in a silver ice bucket. It was a large formal room, but only the portion near the fireplace was lighted, leaving the majority of it in shadows. In the quietness the crackle of the flames sounded loud to Jane's ears.

She went to the fireplace and held her hands toward the warmth, not because she was cold but because that seemed preferable to sitting primly on the stiff brocaded furniture. She didn't know exactly what she had expected tonight, but not this sense of walking into a stage set. The feeling of unreality grew as James opened the bottle of wine, poured each of them a glass, and then walked over to the fireplace, a glass in each hand.

She took the glass, aware of her heartbeat as a definite thump in her chest. "Well, James, what shall we drink to?" she challenged him, holding the glass up. To her own ears she could hear the nervousness beneath the effort at bravado.

James smiled, the perfect host. "You're my guest, Jane. You make the toast, and I'll drink to it." As adroit with words as he was nimble on his feet, James had danced out of reach, just as he had always been able to do when she dared take the offensive, hoping to take him off guard.

Filled with a grudging admiration long-since familiar, Jane lifted the fragile-stemmed goblet higher and gazed into the pale golden liquid, searching her thoughts, only to discover that proposing a toast suddenly wasn't a game of wits or a contest. She wanted to say something honest and meaningful about the two of them being there together on this night. James would be leaving soon, perhaps tomorrow. After this summer she would be leaving Islesboro, too, entering a whole new phase of her life. Their paths weren't likely to cross in the future. Surprising how poignant that thought was.

"To us, James . . . *now*." Jane raised her glass to her lips and watched him over the rim. When it was evident that he didn't intend to drink to her toast, she lowered the glass again, disappointed and vaguely reproachful.

"James, is it asking too much of you to forget about

the past just for an hour or two? Can't we just erase
the things we said and did to each other eons ago,
pretend none of it happened, and think about now?"

James set his glass on the veined marble mantel-
piece that one of his ancestors had had imported from
Italy, as if to emphasize the utter impossibility of his
drinking to her toast. With one elbow propped on the
mantel and the other hand thrust into his pocket, he
looked at Jane, shaking his head disbelievingly.

"You make it sound so easy, just a matter of
'cooperating.' *Just put the past behind you, James,*" he
mocked, and then straightened suddenly, his face
darkening with anger. "Jane, just what the hell do you
think I've been trying to do the last"—he bit back the
descriptive obscenity that came to his lips—"six
years?" Jane stared into the blazing darkness of his
eyes, mesmerized into dumbness by his violent emotion. Seeing her horrified expression, James muttered
a curse under his breath and strode away from her to
the very edge of the lighted portion of the room,
where he wheeled around to face her, more com-
posed.

"Don't misunderstand, Jane. Tonight—the 'now'
you want me to drink to—is something I've waited for
years and years to happen. For you to come here to
me like this, it's the same as having a prize that's been
up on a limb, forever out of reach, suddenly drop into
my lap." He took a step nearer so that Jane could see
the harsh cast of his features more clearly. She was
sure she had never been so humiliated in her entire
life.

"I think what you're trying to tell me, James, is that
a 'prize' is only worth pursuing when it's out of reach.
Isn't that right?" She threw her head back proudly,

gathering force as she continued. "Well, I'd like to remind you that I never asked to be any damned prize, in the first place! And you seem to be jumping to a hell of a lot of conclusions." Jane's hands were shaking so hard that she spilled part of her wine as she set her goblet on the mantel. "Furthermore, I don't have to take your insults—I'm leaving right this moment!

She had barely gotten the last angry word out before James was moving with his lightning quickness and was there to keep her from carrying out her intention. He held her by her upper arms, his body close to hers but not quite touching. Jane's heart lurched automatically with the old feeling of helpless panic until it rapidly sank in that James wasn't actually keeping her there with brute physical force. It was the pure naked longing in his face that held her rooted to the spot, not even trying to escape him, because the same longing trembled inside her.

"James?" She spoke his name with uncertainty, raising a glimmer of hope and extinguishing it at one and the same time. Any sharing between James and herself, tonight or any other night, was doomed before it could be born. The realization brought deep sadness that dulled the golden luminescence of her eyes as she looked into his.

"Don't leave. Stay with me." The low, anguished plea was just barely audible. Jane closed her eyes against the dark urgency in his eyes and then felt the touch of his hands framing her face. Slowly she expelled her breath, releasing with it every shred of resistance, every reservation posed by judgment and common sense. When she felt the heat of his breath fanning her face and knew that he was about to kiss her, she tilted her head back in a response that was totally instinctive, as was the great gathering of anticipation inside her. This was meant to be, she thought as James's lips covered hers.

After that Jane didn't think at all. There was no sense of compromise at staying, perhaps because it seemed that volition was not involved at all. That afternoon she had thought of herself and James as two cosmic bodies on a collision course. Now she was caught up in the inevitability of submitting at long last to that deep attraction that burned between herself and James through the years.

Jane had never known such arousal before. The fever of desire that James awakened in her with the caresses of his hands and mouth and tongue destroyed her inhibitions. She wanted him to know what intense pleasure he gave her, and she wanted to give him that pleasure too. As she touched his body in the boldness of passion, each stroke was a discovery that she had always wanted to touch him thus. There were no surprises. Even when she had hated James and considered him her arch enemy, she had admired his physical beauty. Unwillingly she had been laying the groundwork for the sensual joy of caressing his hard musculature with her palms, of tasting his smooth brown skin with her lips and tongue.

They made love on the floor in front of the fireplace, the priceless old rug providing little softness but a rich background for their naked bodies in the flickering light.

"James, you're so beautiful," Jane told him, running her hands over the breadth of his shoulders and down his back. "Did you know that I always thought that, even when we were enemies?"

"I was never your enemy, Jane, never," James whispered, kissing her breasts, her stomach, her thighs, exploring every curve and most intimate crevice with his hands.

"But you *did* know, didn't you?" she persisted, stroking his chest and then pressing her lips against the hardness.

James groaned and stopped a moment, grabbing her head and holding it against him. "I knew." Then he was plunged back again into his own private blend of heaven and hell. "You're mine," he murmured in a voice that held both joy and torment. "You're mine . . . you're *mine.*"

When the tumult in his loins threatened to explode him into a thousand bits, James took her, not quickly, but slowly and deliberately, extending the moment of possession. His eyes glowed with exultation as he crouched before her parted thighs, poised to enter her. A provocative little movement of his hips teased her with the knowledge that with one surge he could be inside her.

"James—" She spoke his name half in command and half in plea.

"Tell me you want me, Jane," he ordered, the anticipation almost more than he could bear. The bottle he drank from tonight was the finest one in the cellar, and though he had a raging thirst, he wanted to hold the exquisite liquid on his tongue, taste every last nuance of the flavor.

"You know I want you," she chided him tenderly, and smiled at him, lifting her arms as though she would gather him to her.

James looked down at the juncture where his body met hers and watched as with a thrust of his hips, he pushed inside of the wet velvet darkness. Jane drew in her breath sharply with the pleasure of their union and watched an expression like pain grip his face.

"Oh, God, no," James muttered, going rigid.

He was like a superb sculpture depicting an agonizing struggle for control. Jane watched him in fascination, taking pleasure in the flicker of the firelight over his hard naked form. And then he relaxed on top of her, having conquered the convulsive surge of passion.

"You're going to have it all, Jane," he murmured, stroking slowly and deeply inside her. "Remember, I promised you that."

And he kept his promise, raising her to a level of sensation that went beyond anything she had ever known and then to a climax that was not a single cataclysmic explosion like a stroke of lightning but more like a clap of thunder that jarred loud and then rumbled on and on in what seemed an unending series of reverberations, finally dying away and leaving total quiet that was not emptiness but satiation.

"I never knew it could be like that," she told James afterward. They lay side by side, shoulders and hips touching. The revelation bordered on a breach of loyalty to Terry, and a few minutes later, when she was less vulnerable, she probably wouldn't have said it.

James's silence came as a disappointment. She raised herself up and looked down at his face, expecting to see cynicism or at least a shuttered expression. Instead, he looked devastated, as though he simply hadn't been able to collect himself sufficiently to say anything. Gratitude that what had happened meant something to him, too, and a tenderness that she didn't understand welled up in Jane. The latter especially was an emotion she had never expected to feel toward James, the invincible.

"You're a wonderful lover, James," she said softly, stroking her fingertips lightly along his chest and watching in fascination as the smooth hard flesh quivered. "I'm not sorry. Are you?"

"Why should I be sorry?" he countered, and rose from the floor with the effortless coordination she had been admiring all these years. Taking her wineglass over to the table where the bottle nested in the ice bucket, he filled it and carried it back to where she now sat on the carpet, watching his movements with uncertainty.

"Thanks." She took a sip, thinking that he would get his own glass and join her, but instead he began to get dressed. Disappointed as well as hurt that he was clearly in such a hurry to disrupt the intimacy between them, Jane got to her feet, too, and deposited her glass on the mantel again while she retrieved her underwear. Had she said something wrong?

"James, you do believe me, don't you?" she asked awkwardly, dressing. He was already zipping his beltless slacks and sitting down on the edge of the sofa to put on his socks.

"Believe you about what? That you're not sorry we made love or that I pass the test as a lover?"

The edge in his voice brought her movements to a halt. She stood holding the front clasp of her bra together, watching him as he thrust his feet into leather loafers and stood abruptly.

"Why, either one . . . both." Jane wasn't any less puzzled about his behavior, but she was becoming less patient with it. "Do you believe me?" When he didn't answer, Jane stared at him. "James, what reason could I possibly have for lying to you, about anything?"

He shrugged and then walked over to the fireplace, where he took his glass of wine from the mantel and sipped from it.

"Who am I to fathom your reasons?" From his tone of voice Jane was left to conclude that her reasons didn't matter to him one way or the other. He seemed to be waiting for her to finish getting dressed and then be on her way. It was a most demeaning situation for Jane as well as one that totally eluded her understanding. Minutes ago she hadn't felt any embarrassment at being naked in front of him. Now she picked up her dress and held it in front of her, like a shield, intensely aware of his glance as his eyes went over her, from mussed hair to bare feet.

"James, why don't you stop this little guessing game and tell me exactly what you have on your mind?" she suggested with a proud toss of her head. "After that I'll be going, and we can both just chalk this up as a mistake."

His mouth twisted cynically. "I thought you just said you weren't sorry."

"That was before you tried to make me feel like a prostitute!" Shaking with anger, Jane couldn't seem to get her arms through the sleeves of the dress so that she could pull it over her head. Finally she had the dress on and was struggling with the zipper when James's words started sinking in. It was his tone at first that surprised her and elicited her attention. She looked over and saw that he had half-turned away from her and stood with an elbow propped on the mantel and his head braced against his cupped hand.

"How the hell do you think this situation makes *me* feel?" Mixed in with the bitterness was a fatigue that matched the sag in his shoulders. "It's not all that flattering to be sized up for a fool, you know. I come back here after six years and both you and the dear aunt who could never give me the time of day greet me with open arms." His effort at a laugh was harsh and forced. "In your case, literally, need I add? Do you really think I'm too damned stupid not to see through the sudden change in attitude?" He gave his head a violent shake and continued in a bitter, wondering voice. "And the pure hell of it is that even though I can see the trap yawning a mile wide, I'm still tempted to walk right into it with my eyes open."

For several seconds Jane just stared at him, inundated by hot waves of fury and shame that she feared couldn't ever be adequately conveyed with either words or actions. *The nerve of him! The unmitigated gall!* How could he possibly believe that what had happened between them just now was all part of a scheme to entrap him?

Somehow she managed to finish zipping the dress, retrieve her panty hose, crush them into a filmy ball, and jam her bare feet into her shoes. Fleetingly she considered leaving without a word, but then her pride demanded some parting remarks. She faced James with her head high and her shoulders held erect. He had straightened and was watching her, standing evenly balanced on legs slightly apart, his arms down at his sides in a stance that should have been relaxed but wasn't.

"Jane—"

"Don't you 'Jane' me!" she bit out between

clenched teeth. "Don't you dare say another word to me, James Patton, *ever!* For your information, this is one trap that is officially 'closed' and the 'bait' is about to *lea—*" Her voice played traitor and broke at a point when she hadn't nearly said all that she wanted to say. Suddenly she had her hands full fighting the onslaught of tears and knew as she blinked hard and swallowed that her predicament must be providing him no end of pleasure.

"Jane—" James moved quickly, covering the distance between them and coming to stand in front of her. His hands closed around her shoulders gently until she tried to jerk free of him, and then not so gently, more like a vise holding her. The pressure was all the excuse she needed to let the tears flow. She brought her hands up to cover her face at the same time that James drew her against him.

"I'm crying because I'm *mad,* damn it!" she gulped against his chest. "That's the only reason! Don't you go saying you're sorry, either, because you meant every word you said."

James held her, waiting for the tears to subside, saying nothing as she had commanded him. When she pushed against him, his arms loosened but his hands came up again to hold her shoulders.

"Jane, I want to try to explain—" he began hesitantly.

"There's nothing to explain," she broke in, trying to pull free of him. "Now, let me go!" What began as an effort to resist his restraining hold turned into a full-fledged attack. She pounded at him with her fists and tried to kick him, her level of frustration and fury rising until she was nearly insensible. *"I hate you,*

James Patton! Hate you, hate you, hate you!" she heard herself shrieking, and somehow the sound of her own hysterical voice brought her back to sanity. Her resistance crumpled.

"Damn you, why don't you let me go?" she whimpered, looking up at him, shame and hurt written all over her face.

James dropped his arms away from her and stepped back. "I won't force you to stay, Jane," he said quietly, "but I'm asking you to. Please—there're some things I need to say."

Jane felt battered. What she wanted more than anything else was to creep off somewhere alone. It was the instinct nature had given to an injured animal.

"Okay, James, say whatever it is you want to say," she said dully, crossing her arms across her chest. "No, I don't want any more wine," she put in crossly when he started toward the mantel and her glass of wine.

He stopped short. "Will you at least sit down?"

The faint desperation in the request roused Jane a little out of her own absorption with herself. James was obviously dreading this "explanation," whatever it was. In spite of herself Jane felt the beginnings of curiosity. She went over to the sofa and sat at one end, noticing idly that she still had her panty hose crushed into a ball in her hand.

"All right, James, I'm sitting," she prompted him coolly.

He hesitated and then came and sat a few feet away from her. After a sideways glance he fixed his gaze, too, upon the remnants of the fire. They were like two people keeping a vigil.

"I came back here this summer, for the first time in six years, to prove something to myself," James began with the air of one forcing a confidence upon a stranger who might not be particularly interested. "It was a kind of test I had decided I should be able to pass by this time. I wanted to come back to this place—see you—and feel nothing. We anchored the boat that day that I swam ashore and I sat for over an hour, watching for some sign of you with the binoculars." With a gorgeous woman sitting next to him in the cockpit of the yacht and making jealous comments.

"The moment you walked out on the terrace, I knew. Nothing had changed." James's tone conveyed his bafflement at the unwanted discovery. "The same old attraction was still there, after six years of not seeing you or hearing your voice or even letting myself think of you. And I didn't understand why it was there any more than I ever had."

He got up, retrieved his wineglass, and went to refill it. "Change your mind?" he asked over his shoulder.

"Yes."

Silence curled through the room. Sounds so muted that they ordinarily would have passed unnoticed were deafeningly loud to Jane's heightened senses: the gurgle of wine filling the crystal bowls of the wineglasses, the quick tread of James's shoes on the rug, the sofa cushion receiving his weight.

James slumped back, one ankle resting on the knee of the opposite leg. He sipped his wine and picked up the monologue, still directing his gaze at the fireplace. Jane, though, had shifted slightly sideways so that she could see his profile.

"I swam over, half hoping that seeing you close up would show me my first reaction was wrong. Walking across the grass toward you, I had this awful sensation of déjà vu, and sure enough, almost immediately we were playing out the same old scene. It was that day I decided to sell this cottage. I was admitting to myself something that came as a bitter pill: I was licked. I had lost at a game I'd never really understood or figured out how to play.

"That day you walked in on me in the library, I intended to pick out the few things I'd keep and then get the hell out of here. I didn't even plan to stay overnight." At her sound of surprise, he rolled his head sideways to look at her. "I should have stuck to that original plan, but you took me completely off guard—the prey stalking the hunter." His grunt was ironic.

"I had my suspicions right off, and they seemed confirmed when you ushered me into my aunt's house and she dripped honey all over me. I told myself I'd be a fool not to take what was being offered me. Then I'd be on my way." He sat up straighter and slid closer to her so that he could pick up the hand that rested on her thigh. He brought the hand up to his face and nuzzled it along his cheekbone. "It wasn't that easy though."

Jane was torn with conflict, drawn to him and yet still distrustful, afraid to open herself up to further hurt and insult. One instinct made her want to disengage her hand while a dissenting one urged her to slide closer to him.

"James, I won't deny that my aunt might have some hope that a match between you and me would solve all our financial problems. I won't even deny that the thought has crossed *my* mind, but I didn't come over here that day to lure you into a trap. I came over to thank you for sending Abe and his grandson to work on the grounds and also to find out if you were the buyer the real estate agent had mentioned the day before when he brought the papers that Aunt Lottie refused to sign." James had lowered her hand to his thigh and was looking down at it, so she really couldn't read his expression.

"Believe me, I had *no* intention whatever of suggesting we see each other that evening." She paused, recapturing the scene in her mind. "It was pure impulse. Suddenly I just didn't want to walk out and leave things the way they were. I *wanted* to see you again. You spoke just now of my 'attraction' for you. Well, I think you always knew you had a certain fascination for me, too, and maybe I felt I was free to explore it." She moved her hand ever so slightly on his thigh, feeling the corded muscles and then the reflex that rippled through them.

"You enjoy your sense of power over me, don't you, Jane?" he asked softly, leaning toward her so that their faces were only inches apart. She held her breath, her lips slightly parted as he brought his mouth to hers but only teased with a provocative brushing contact that make her want to clasp his head and force him closer.

"No more than you enjoy your power over me." Her lips grazed his as she formed the words, and he drew back. She could see his chest rising and falling with his breathing. "I don't know what more I can say to convince you, James. Either you believe me or you don't." Her own heart was beating fast, too, making her sound a little breathless.

"Even if I do believe you, Jane, it's more complicated than that." He got up from the sofa and went back over to the table with the wine bottle, but left his half-filled glass on the tray. Instead of returning to the sofa, he went to stand by the fireplace.

Jane got up too. "It's Terry, isn't it?" He didn't have to say anything. The answer was there on his face. "You can't forget the fact that I married him and not you. James, you can't be jealous of a dead man!"

He shrugged. "None of this is a matter of choice, Jane. Haven't you understood anything I've told you? I don't want to be jealous of my dead cousin. I don't want it to matter that if he were alive, you wouldn't be here with me. You'd be with him. I don't want it to pass through my mind that no matter what happens between you and me, he was the one you always defended and—loved." The last word stuck in James's throat and came out harsh.

Jane shook her head helplessly, wishing there were some easy answers she could give him, but there were none. Nothing could change the fact that she *had* chosen Terry over James. She couldn't even tell James that given the same choice she would make a different decision.

"Things happened the way they did! For all kinds of reasons. Terry always needed me. You never seemed to need anyone. I'm beginning to see now that your tough shell was a kind of defense against the world. Underneath you might have wanted love and friendship, but you never showed that to me, James—or to Terry. You were mean to him for no good reason."

She turned away, breathing out a dispirited sigh. Emotionally this had been one of the most exhausting evenings of her life. She felt totally drained. "I think I'd better go now."

James made no effort to stop her. She left the room quickly, not daring to look back.

Chapter Six

Jane had trouble falling asleep that night. Her mind kept going over the recent scenes between James and herself, beginning with the day he'd swum over from the yacht and taken her totally by surprise. She went over each conversation, trying to remember exactly what *she* had said and *he* had said and the exact tones of their voices and possible nuances.

Then she went back into time and resurrected old scenes with the two cousins and herself, looking upon the interchanges now with her new insight into James, who apparently had not been as impervious to words and attitudes as he had seemed. There was no denying that the atmosphere at his aunt's summer cottage had not been hospitable toward James. The relationships among the Pattons had been well established by the time Jane came into their lives. She had unquestioningly adopted the attitudes taught her about the relatives next door. Perhaps that had been a short-coming, but one easily explained under the circum-stances. James had couched the situation in blunt but accurate terms that first day she had met him: Jane was the "new poor relation."

Her mother had conveyed her sense of terror at being at the mercy of the world after her husband died, leaving her and her daughter penniless. It was made plain to the ten-year-old Jane that the wealthy cousin who was taking her mother and herself in was their means of survival. It was a situation that called for Jane to please her benefactor. Then Lottie had proceeded to take charge of Jane's life, sending her to the best schools, providing her with a lavish and beautiful wardrobe. Lottie had pre-empted the role of Jane's mother, who had seemed willing to relinquish it in Jane's best interest.

The instinct to please had been reinforced through the years. Jane could look back and see that, but it didn't negate the fact of Lottie's generosity *or* the deep bonds of affection that had bound Lottie, Terry, and Jane together. They were a "family," though not a conventional one. But for Lottie's money, Jane and Terry might have grown up feeling more like brother and sister, but they had both gone to expensive boarding schools and seen each other mainly at holi-days and during the summer. There had been between them the closeness and ease of long-time companions, but they had not been siblings.

Jane couldn't remember the exact moment or occa-sion when Terry had announced his intention to marry her someday. Strangely enough, she couldn't even recall how she had felt when the eventuality of marriage to Terry was introduced into her life, like a minor color in the tapestry of the present. Certainly she hadn't rebelled against the idea. It had been flattering to be "marked out" in advance, and the future was years away. She enjoyed the air of special-ness it gave her to be unofficially engaged. Her girlfriends all made quite a production of being envi-ous when they would meet Terry, who had an aesthet-ic handsomeness entirely appropriate for a young man devoted to art.

Mentally Jane stood Terry and James side by side the way they had looked six years ago. Terry had been tall, thin, and fair-skinned with fine-textured blond hair that emphasized rather than hid the contours of his skull. A swath of hair always fell across his forehead. His hands looked awkward, as though he didn't quite know what to do with them when they weren't holding a paintbrush. The nearest he came to engaging in physical exertion as an adult was walking through the woods. As a child his mother had cur-tailed his physical activities out of a sense of protec-tiveness. He and Jane had spent hours during the summer playing croquet, a "pansy" sport according to his cousin, James, Terry's antithesis in every way.

James looked like a Patton, with dark hair and dark eyes that were never opaque, even when he was guarded. They gleamed and penetrated with the quick workings of his sharp intelligence. Not as tall as Terry, James had a superb body, supple and fit, with no bulging muscle definition. Even when he was standing perfectly still there was always that suggestion of readiness, as though his muscles could take a message from his brain and go into action instantly.

Jane saw him the way he had looked tonight, naked

with the firelight flickering over his body. The image excited her. Loyalty to Terry couldn't prevent her from admitting the truth: Even though she had loved Terry, she had never felt the same tense awareness, the same sexual excitement with him that she felt with James. She had told James the truth tonight after they had made love. What she had experienced with him transcended anything she'd ever known before. True, she had made love with Terry only after they were married. Perhaps some change had taken place within her to unleash her sensuality. Perhaps she would feel that same sexual intensity with another man sometime in the future.

Somehow she doubted it.

The next morning she slept late, awaking just in time to dress and drive to the village. She was glad to be scheduled at the crafts co-op that morning and hoped that they would be busy. She didn't want to think about James and last night.

But by eleven-thirty not a single person had wandered in. Jane worked on her new cross-stitch design and found that her needlework was failing her today: The sense of restlessness with which she had awakened didn't go away. Close concentration didn't bring the desired mindless tranquility.

When the bell over the door jangled she looked up to see a young woman about her own age enter. Smartly dressed in a sporty red pants suit, her platinum blond hair just brushing her shoulders in a hair style that was casual perfection, Jane knew on sight that the lone customer was part of the wealthier summer set. She looked familiar and yet Jane couldn't place her.

At the sight of Jane, who had risen and walked toward the center of the large display room, the young woman stopped and stared.

"Jane? Is that really you?"

The sound of her voice brought recognition. "Susan McGraw! No wonder I didn't recognize you! You alternated between being a brunette and a redhead in college, but never a blonde!"

The two former friends grinned delightedly at each other and then took the remaining steps separating them from an enthusiastic embrace.

"What on *earth*—" they began simultaneously and then broke down into giggles before continuing in deliberate unison, "are you doing here?"

"I live here," Jane explained matter-of-factly.

Susan had a look of intense concentration as she searched her memory. "You dropped out of college at the end of our junior year and got married. Ah, yes, now I'm beginning to remember."

She was too tactful to continue, but Jane knew that Susan was probably recalling the gossip that had undoubtedly buzzed in their social circles at that time.

"I married Terry—you met him."

"Of course, the artist! Tall, blond, poetic-looking." Susan's first surprise was fading and her memory was supplying details that made her slightly ill at ease because she didn't want to do or say anything to embarrass Jane. Heiress to a textile fortune, she was ill equipped to even imagine what it was like to lose all one's money and have to drop out of social circulation. "Jane, I'm so happy to see you again. I hope you're glad to see me too," Susan implored awkwardly.

Jane was touched by her old school friend's sensitivity. "I am glad to see you, Susan," she said warmly, giving Susan another little hug. "I know you'll have trouble believing this, but life does go on without trips to Europe and the latest Paris fashions." She laughed teasingly. "I can see you're unconvinced." Briefly she summarized the past six years, her face saddening as she told of Terry's death.

"Oh, Jane, I'm sorry . . ." Susan murmured.

"So what about you? What's happened in your life since I saw you last—" Jane stopped short, appalled at herself for not remembering. It was Susan's turn to put her at ease.

"It's okay, Jane. I don't mind talking about it. I didn't have Mike's baby. I went ahead and had an abortion, the way my parents wanted." The glaze of emotion in her blue eyes brought back to Jane the constant dread of those several days when she hadn't even dared leave Susan long enough to attend class. She had been afraid Susan would choose suicide as the way out of her problem. It hadn't been just the unwanted pregnancy that had upset Susan's mental and emotional balance, but the belief that she had caused Mike's death. Unlike herself, he hadn't survived the collision of her new sports car with an oncoming vehicle. She had been high on youth and alcohol and driving much too fast.

"Jane, you were a true friend to me at a time in my life when I needed a friend. And you never breathed a word to anyone. There have been times the past few years when it would cross my mind that I'd like to see you again and thank you, but, of course, I never did. One tends to get so busy. Time passes. . . ."

Jane added her agreement to that last sentiment and then smiled broadly. "Don't we sound like a couple of octogenarians though?" Susan giggled, and the two women looked at each other, feeling incredibly close. An expression of regret flitted across Susan's face.

"Oh, damn! Here I've just found you, and I have to leave in a few hours. It's nothing I can put off either. My parents are having a big anniversary bash in Monte Carlo. But at least we could have lunch together, couldn't we?" When Jane showed some hesitation, Susan rushed on. "Oh, *please!* I'll call over to the inn right now and make sure they have a quiet table for us in the corner. You'll be my guest—I insist upon it!"

Jane was unable to resist her entreaty. For the second day in a row Lottie would be left to her own devices for preparing a midday meal, but if Jane didn't take this time with Susan, she might not have another chance. There was no telling when their paths would cross again.

"We'll have to wait until my relief arrives." Jane glanced at her watch. "That should be in thirty minutes or so."

Susan was jubilant. "Great! This is such an unexpected treat! Do you have a telephone here I can use?" She looked around. "What are you doing here anyway? I don't remember you as the artsy-craftsy type."

"I wasn't. There's a telephone back here."

Susan called the inn and, using the name of her hostess on the island, easily disposed of any problems in getting a lunch reservation at the last minute. Then she turned her full attention to Jane's needlework on display.

"God, these are *fabulous,* Jane! And you don't use a pattern at all? You make up the designs yourself?"

Jane explained that she got ideas from various sources, including illustrations in some old books on the history of needlework she'd discovered in Lottie's book collection at the cottage. Once she'd become adept at all the stitches, she was able to adapt any painting or photograph that struck her fancy.

"To that extent, you can say I 'make up' the designs myself," she ended modestly.

"I'm impressed," Susan declared. "I've never even managed to make a decent job of the McGraw Learner's Sampler. My father had the harebrained inspiration one time to use me in an ad with my own finished product!"

Susan's words were a reminder of what Jane had forgotten: Her family were the McGraws of the McGraw Manufacturing Company, which manufactured needlework supplies and a large variety of embroidery and needlepoint kits. Jane remembered the suggestion made by a customer some days ago, that she should sell some of her original designs to a kit manufacturer. Then to her amazement, Susan was popping out with the same idea.

"I'll bet my father would be interested in seeing some of these." Before Jane could demur, Susan shrewdly read her old friend's expression and challenged her reservation. "I know what you're thinking, Jane. You don't want to 'use' your friendship with me. Well, whether you like to believe it or not, half the business deals in the world—maybe more—depend on personal contacts." She was struck with a sudden impulse that obviously pleased her. "I'm going to buy one of your pieces. Hmmm, I'll take *that* sampler. I'll take it with me to Monte Carlo and show it to Father. I can assure you that if he doesn't think my idea is a good one, it won't go any further. My father is too good a businessman to take anybody's suggestion, including mine, if he doesn't think it'll make money for his company."

A skirmish of wills followed with Jane trying to give Susan the piece of needlework she had chosen and Susan insisting that she would pay for it. Susan won, mainly because Jane knew the money meant nothing to Susan, while Jane needed every penny she could get.

"There." Susan tucked her parcel under her arm. "Another thing, before I forget. I want to get your mailing address and telephone number."

Jane jotted the information on a pad and handed the page to Susan. "You can reach me here through the end of August." When she had to admit to Susan that she didn't know herself where she'd be after that time, Susan was intrigued, but the arrival of Jane's relief postponed further private conversation.

Later, over lunch, when Jane had explained the whole situation at some length, Susan sat back in her chair, thoughtful. "Hmmm, you want to move to a warmer climate, which means south or west, right? I gather you'd like to get to know your mother again, but keep a certain distance too." Jane nodded, appreciative of Susan's quick grasp. "Jane, I have a condo right on the coast, just north of Fort Lauderdale, that you'd be more than welcome to use for as long as you wanted." She grimaced, but Jane didn't miss the sadness in her eyes. "It was a hideaway place for Lynn, my first husband, and me. Oh, yes," she continued cynically, replying to Jane's unasked questions, "I've been married *twice* and am in the process of divorcing my second husband right now.

"About this condo," she went on briskly. "It's just sitting there. I have no intention of either selling or leasing it, for the present. It would please me no end, Jane, if you'd make use of it."

There was no doubt that Susan's offer was a sincere one. Jane felt excitement growing inside her at the realization that here was her opportunity to give concrete definition to those vague but determined plans for her future. If she accepted Susan's offer, at the end of August she would be going not "somewhere" but to a specific locale, Fort Lauderdale, Florida.

"If my mother-in-law does come to her senses, is it all right—"

"Of course," Susan broke in before Jane could even finish the question. "It's settled then?" she prompted.

Jane had to hold back a wave of panic. "Yes. If you're really sure."

"I'm sure. Here, let me give you the key right now since I'm leaving the country and don't know for certain when I'll be back. I'll have my father's secretary send a letter to the manager of the complex just to make sure you don't have any trouble. If you decide to go on down before the end of August, Jane, feel free."

Susan took the key off a gold keychain with a little diamond horseshoe and handed it to Jane, who gazed down at it in the palm of her hand.

"I have this strange feeling that your walking into the co-op today was fate," she said slowly, looking up. "Now I have a place to go. As soon as I get a job and can find something of my own I can afford, I'll return the key. Susan, maybe someday I can do something for you."

"You already have," Susan reminded gently. "I doubt I'd be here today if you hadn't stuck to me like a shadow right after Mike was killed. And don't bother to return the key. Just leave it with the management office. I've been carrying it around with me too long."

Jane's exhilaration deflated abruptly an hour later when she arrived back at the cottage and found James's Ferrari parked in front of the entrance. Inside, he and Lottie were seated in the living room. As Jane entered, taking in with a glance the silver coffee service and porcelain coffee cups, she had the distinct impression that the conversation had ceased with the sounds of her arrival.

"Why, James, what a surprise," she said coolly, not liking the feeling of being an intruder. Her eyes let him know she intended to find out at once what he was up to.

"James and I have been having a delightful little chat, haven't we, James?" Lottie gushed.

"Have you now?" Jane lifted one eyebrow and held James's gaze. He looked back steadily with not a flicker of expression.

"My aunt and I have been talking," he said evenly.

Jane pressed her lips together to keep back an indignant retort. They'd been "talking," all right. He'd been conducting his own little investigation to dig out the plot he suspected his aunt and Jane had cooked up to entrap him!

"We've been waiting for you, Jane, dear." A forced

note in Lottie's cheerful voice caught Jane's attention at once. It was a silent plea.

"I'm here now, Aunt Lottie."

"James has expressed an interest in seeing Terry's paintings. I told him you would show them to him." Even in the interest of ingratiating herself with James, Lottie couldn't face going into her son's sanctum again.

Jane's eyes flew to James. *What in hell is going on here!* she demanded silently.

"Will you show them to me?" James put the matter squarely between Jane and himself, making it plain that she could refuse and that would be the end of it.

Jane stared back at him, remembering the tortured admission he had made to her the night before: He was jealous of his dead cousin. Now he was asking to see Terry's paintings. It didn't make sense!

Without a word she turned to lead him back to Terry's studio. She walked fast, aware of him right behind her. At the door she stopped and turned to face him.

"James—this doesn't *feel* right." She could read in his eyes that he understood perfectly her deep reluctance and could offer no reassurance. He stood there, waiting once again for her to decide. "I don't understand why you want to see his paintings." Jane sighed and opened the door.

The long, high-ceilinged room extended the depth of the house. Originally it had been two rooms and a porch, but Lottie had had it renovated according to Terry's own specifications. It was flooded with natural light, its many windows uncovered, their blankness contributing to the overall stark bareness.

Since Terry's death Jane had entered the studio periodically to clean it, but had left it virtually unchanged otherwise. The strong sense of Terry's presence saddened her but also made her feel close to him, as though he were not totally lost to her. Today, though, she was aware only of James. As he took several steps beyond the threshold and looked around, Jane realized for the first time that James was forcing himself, for whatever reasons, through what was a terrible ordeal for him. *He didn't really want to see Terry's paintings!* The perception canceled out her instinctive obligation to shield Terry from an unsympathetic inspection of his artwork. Instead, she wished that she could make this easier for James.

"Terry practically lived in this room," she pointed out conversationally, gesturing toward the studio couch along one wall. But James barely seemed to hear her. He took several more steps inside and looked slowly around at the unframed canvases, most of them quite large, hung haphazardly around the room. Dozens of others were propped at an angle against the walls. The one Terry had been working on when he took ill was still in place on the easel. To Jane it represented a great violet tornado gathering destructive force as it whirled along.

"You're surprised, aren't you?" she asked quietly.

James knew that *surprised* didn't even come close to expressing the way he felt. He was overwhelmed. In canvas after canvas the boldness in color and technique was combined with an exquisite subtlety that made the muscles in his throat tighten with emotion. He felt he was looking into the artist's very soul—*his cousin Terry's soul.* James was no art expert by far, but he knew he was looking at the evidence of a monumental talent. The realization made him sick inside. God help him, at least he could be honest with himself. He had brazened his way into this studio hoping to find the work of a dilettante, not a gifted artist. And Jane wanted to know if he was "surprised."

"He confined his work to abstract art?" James walked over to stand in front of the easel, not to get a closer look at the unfinished painting but to conceal his expression from Jane.

"He began to paint in this style when he was living in Paris. After he came home he destroyed everything he'd done before in what he called his 'infancy of realism.' Its only importance, he said, was to allow him to get beyond it." Jane laughed apologetically. "To tell you the truth, I never had the faintest idea what he meant. I liked his other paintings." She hesitated. "I think I was able to understand them better than these."

"Didn't he ever try to arrange with an art gallery to show his work?"

"Not to my knowledge. He never went anywhere. He was perfectly content to stay right here on the estate and paint."

With two doting women at his beck and call. James had seen enough, more than enough. He needed to get out of there and fast. The crimsons and purples and overripe pinks were closing in all around him. He felt as if he were drowning in a sea stained with the violent hues of a tropical sunset.

"To each his own, I suppose." Desperate, James glanced at his watch as though he had an appointment to keep. Then he realized the gesture was wasted since he still had his back to her. "Well, thank you for showing me—" Wheeling around, he discovered that Jane had drifted up close behind him. He reached out and grabbed her upper arms as though to stop himself from charging over her.

"Are you all right?" Jane asked in concern when she saw the unhealthy pallor of his face.

It was Jane's turn to follow behind James. He wasted no time retracing his steps through the house. Only when he had reached the front entrance and stepped outside did he stop.

"You're leaving?" Jane addressed the question to his back from the open door. She wanted to know what he had thought of Terry's paintings, and yet she lacked the courage to ask.

James felt better with his lungs full of fresh air. He took in another deep breath and turned around to face her. "Have dinner with me tonight?" He took a step nearer, as though pressing his case.

"James, do you think—I mean, after last night—" Jane broke off with a sigh, letting her lifted shoulders and her face finish out her reservation.

"Yes, I do think—especially after last night," he came back in a quick monotone. "Look, all I'm asking you is to have dinner with me. A meal, conversation, and nothing more, if that's the way you want it." He paused and his features hardened cynically. "There're some matters of importance we need to discuss."

Jane crossed her arms across her chest and leaned against the doorframe. "James, I don't know what there is at this point that you and I would need to talk about. Hasn't everything already been said?"

"You know it hasn't." The terse contradiction matched the hardness in his face.

Jane threw up her hands helplessly. "James, I don't

know what kind of intrigue you've built up in that suspicious mind of yours now!"

James stepped closer, caught her hands in his, and held them lightly behind her so that her shoulders and breasts were thrust forward. Exerting a light pressure, he pulled her forward until the peaks of her breasts rested lightly against his chest. Looking down at the contact with an absorbed expression and then into her eyes, he suggested mildly, changing the whole tone of the invitation, "Have dinner with me and find out. Hmm?" His hands turned hers loose and came up to frame her face. Then, as though he had lost interest in hearing her answer, he brought his lips to hers and took a deep, quick kiss.

"A meal and conversation—that's what you said, isn't it?" Jane reminded him huskily, balling her hands into fists and keeping them firmly at her back.

James took her lips again in another deep kiss, one that lasted longer but ended as abruptly as the first, leaving her hungry for more. "That's what I said." He murmured the words against her lips, dropped his hands, and stepped back.

Jane felt the powerful magnetic pull between them and had to resist it to keep from being drawn after him. She wanted nothing more than to press close to him again and this time put her arms up around his neck.

He had retreated even farther and was waiting for her answer, one hand on the door of the Ferrari, Jane knew all her initial reservations about seeing him that evening were wellfounded. It was out of the question for the two of them to be just casual friends. The force drawing them together was too strong. And yet a deeper relationship was equally impossible. The past had left scars too deep for James ever to forgive or trust her.

Jane should refuse his invitation . . . and yet she couldn't. The urge to be with him was stronger than the dictates of common sense or the instinct for self-preservation. She rationalized that it had to be the same for him. Did he, like herself, see every meeting between them as possibly their last? That thought brought to mind the surprise encounter with Susan, which she had entirely forgotten in her shock at discovering James here at the cottage talking to Lottie in what had seemed an atmosphere of "collusion," followed by James's totally unexpected and unexplained request to see Terry's paintings. Jane had quite forgotten the key in her handbag up until now.

"Okay, James. Let's do have dinner tonight. I have something exciting to tell you. Something that happened to me today." The sense of wonder at the workings of fate returned, curving her lips into a smile and making her eyes luminous as she looked into a future that promised a new beginning.

James noted the transformation in her face and asked himself if eyes with that clarity and fathomless depth could ever hide an unworthy thought, let alone an out-and-out falsehood?

After he had left, Jane went inside to tell Lottie about the surprise meeting with Susan McGraw. The older woman was no longer in the living room, but Jane noticed that she had left the coffee service and cups, obviously expecting Jane to clean up, as she would do later after she'd talked to Lottie. Now was not the time to make an issue of domestic chores. If Lottie chose to go to Florida with Jane, the two of them would work matters out between them. If Lottie stayed here, she would have to do everything for herself because Jane wouldn't be around to take care of her.

She found her mother-in-law out on the terrace, playing solitaire. When Lottie looked up eagerly, her eyes full of questions that all centered around James, Jane quickly plunged into an account of her surprise reunion with Susan which had ended in Susan's generous offer of the use of her condominium.

"It's empty and waiting for us. I have the key in my purse." Jane made her voice cheerful, as though she hadn't noticed the storm gathering in Lottie's face.

"I have no intention of living in any condominium in Florida, Jane," Lottie announced frostily, and then compressed her lips while she drew in a deep, audible breath before continuing in the same provoked tone. "There's no reason for either of us to have to accept the charity of strangers—"

"Susan isn't a stranger," Jane broke in. "She was one of my best friends in college. I don't consider her offer of the use of her condominium *charity*." Jane took a deep breath to calm herself. It wouldn't do either of them any good for her to get emotional. "Aunt Lottie, please don't misunderstand what I'm going to say. I sincerely hope that you will decide to come with me to Florida, but whether you do or not makes no difference in my own plans. *I* am going." Jane steeled herself against the cold fury that burned in her mother-in-law's eyes.

"What have I ever done to you to make you treat me like this?" Lottie's voice trembled with rage and disbelief. Her face was blotched with patches of crimson, as though anger would pulse the blood right through the pores of her skin. "Have you no feelings of gratitude for what I've done for you? No reverence for my son's memory? *Ahhhhhh—*" Her face constricted horribly as she made a sound of helpless outrage.

Jane watched her in horrified fascination. *Lottie hadn't believed her for a moment, before now, when Jane had said she was going!* Did her mother-in-law really believe that Jane had no say over her own life? Did she think Jane was a puppet with no judgment or will?

"Aunt Lottie, you're being terribly unfair, and you know it! How can you expect me to . . . to *bury* myself here with you? I'm young—*you're* young!" Jane was reassured by the firmness of her own voice. She wouldn't back down no matter how hard Lottie tried to make her feel like an ingrate.

Lottie passed a trembling hand across her face as though to wipe away the accusation and anger. Her whole body sagged momentarily, but then she roused herself out of the apathy that threatened to destroy all hope of dealing with Jane's hardheadedness.

"I'm not asking you to bury yourself here, don't you understand? All it would take from you is the slightest encouragement, and James would marry you. No—listen to what I say." Lottie held up a hand to silence Jane, who had drawn her breath in sharply. "He was always . . . attached to you, and he still is. He is a very wealthy man, Jane. He would make you a good husband. You would have everything you could want." Lottie lifted her head proudly. "As God is my witness, I never thought I would have to speak such a thought aloud to anyone, but it seems you leave me no choice: As James's wife, you could make *my* life easier with no sacrifice to yourself." Her lips tightened bitterly. "But that would never occur to you, I suppose."

Jane was shaking her head so hard, it was making her dizzy. "I just can't believe this! I just can't believe . . ." she murmured and then made the effort to compose herself and marshal her thoughts.

"Aunt Lottie, I don't know how you've allowed yourself to build up this whole make-believe fantasy in your mind, but James has no intention whatever of asking me to marry him. *I* should know. You *must* believe that. James is never, ever, going to make your life easier, Aunt Lottie. As far as he is concerned, he doesn't have a single reason to feel kindly toward you—toward either of us."

Now that she had calmed down, Jane's mind was racing. She was remembering the silence that had fallen when she walked into the living room earlier and discovered Lottie and James, acting like conspirators. Dear God, what had Lottie said to James? No doubt she had confirmed all his suspicions about a plot between the two women to entrap him! Jane's face burned with embarrassment just to think about it. At least tonight she would have a chance to prove all his suspicions wrong. The key to Susan's condominium was tangible proof that Jane meant to leave Islesboro without any help from James and embark on a whole new life of her own. She would show it to him, convince him of her innocence.

Chapter Seven

$\mathcal{T}$hroughout the afternoon, whenever Jane's thoughts would return to the emotionally charged scene between herself and Lottie, she would always reach the same conclusion: During that private conversation with his aunt prior to Jane's return to the cottage, James must have strengthened Lottie's desperate hope that he would marry Jane and provide for Lottie's own well-being. Otherwise, why would Lottie be so *sure?*

Knowing James—or at least the "old" James—Jane could easily believe him capable of playing such a cruel joke on his aunt and enjoying the situation immensely. But Jane wasn't amused. She would find out that evening if her suspicions were true. If they were, she would let James know her low opinion of such shabby behavior on his part.

James picked her up at seven. There was open

approval in his dark eyes as he appraised her appearance, along with a new emotion she identified after a shocked moment as possessiveness. *James was looking at her as though he owned her!* Jane remembered Lottie's certainty that James would marry her if only she played her cards right and didn't spoil things. Had those two actually carried on an open transaction involving Jane, as though she were some item up for barter?

"Have you eaten at that little place in the village, the Blue Heron?" James inquired pleasantly when they were headed along the lane to the highway. The timbre of his voice matched what she had seen in his eyes and sent a strange prickling sensation skimming over the surface of her skin. For a fleeting moment Jane wondered if she could hold her own against the two of them, Lottie and James. They were powerful personalities individually. Together they would be awesome.

"No, I haven't eaten there."

"Good." James reached over and squeezed her hands, which were clasped tightly together in her lap. "Neither have I. We'll take a chance on it, if you're game. I called earlier and made a reservation."

He was taking the simple fact that neither of them had dined in the restaurant and investing it with a significance she perceived at once: Tonight was a new beginning in their relationship and, thus, it should take place in new surroundings. What struck Jane and offended her as well was the undertone of utter certainty that she would concur with whatever he suggested. Consulting her was a mere formality.

"I've heard from several people that the food is quite good." Jane reminded him with the coolness of her tone that she had agreed to dine with him and nothing else. He glanced over at her quickly but made no comment.

During the remainder of the short drive to Dark Harbor neither of them made any attempt at further conversation. Jane had time to doubt her perceptions and wonder if there really had been cause for defensiveness. James might have no more ulterior motive than the wish for the two of them to have a pleasant evening in surroundings that held no past associations.

The Blue Heron was located in a small frame building in the heart of the village. Everything about it made a good impression upon Jane when they entered. The decor was fresh and attractive. The noise level was comfortable, neither too noisy nor oppressively quiet. The waitress who greeted them and showed them to a table was winsomely pretty and seemingly efficient too. When she had taken their order and whisked away, Jane smiled at James across the table.

"Hmm, this is very nice." Her approval held the merest hint of apology for having possibly misjudged him earlier.

"I'm glad you like it," he replied cautiously, biding his time. Seeing the look of possession lurking in the dark depths of his eyes raised a wave of uneasiness inside Jane. To her heightened imagination, the two of them seemed to occupy a small island of privacy, lit by the candle on their table. Its softly flickering light deepened the blue of the tablecloth and cast patterns across James's features. The intimacy was so intense that Jane felt she had to establish a more casual atmosphere if she wanted to maintain her distance from James, if she hoped to retain *control*.

Touching her fingertips to the petals of the daisies in the little bouquet on their table, she commented whimsically, "Fresh flowers . . . that's always a good sign, isn't it?"

"A good sign of what?" James's tone was patient but gently insistent, the force of his personality dragging Jane's gaze up to meet his.

"Why, that the restaurant is likely to be a good one, of course." To fight the magnetic force he was deliberately exerting over her, Jane was about to abandon the effort at casualness and ask him pointblank what he and Lottie had talked about today, but the waitress made a timely interruption, arriving to serve the wine James had ordered in lieu of pre-dinner cocktails. After the tasting ritual had been carried out, she poured the wine and left again.

"That's what I call a 'good sign' . . . a waitress that doesn't feel like she has to make friends with her customers," James commented lightly, and then raised his glass to Jane in a playful salute.

Beguiled into believing that they both were putting off the confrontation that would have to come later, Jane smiled back at him and lifted her glass to her lips. His next words, which were a flagrant violation of the tacit agreement she thought they'd just made, to talk about surface matters and avoid controversy, took her completely off guard.

"What was the exciting news you promised to tell me about tonight?"

Jane choked on the swallow of wine. Putting her glass down, she eyed James accusingly and only became the more irritated when she read his expression. James didn't really think she *had* any genuine "exciting news." He thought they were just playing out a game of cat and mouse, a silly, useless game, in his opinion, but one he would tolerate if she insisted.

"First, I want to know what you and Aunt Lottie talked about before I got home today," she demanded belligerently.

James's eyebrows shot up to express his immediate reaction, skepticism tinged with impatience, but then he shrugged, willing to indulge her. It was obvious from his tone that he was quite sure he wasn't telling Jane anything she didn't already know.

"My aunt called me this morning and asked if I could come over. She didn't mention, of course, that you would be very conveniently absent. We talked about a number of subjects, including her deplorable state of finances—"

"She *called* you and *asked* you to come see her?" Jane broke in incredulously, the outburst prompted not by doubt that he was telling the truth but by amazement and chagrin. How could Lottie go behind Jane's back and put her in this humiliating position?

"James, I didn't know—I swear it! I came home and saw your car parked there and assumed that you had deliberately timed your visit . . ." To Jane's utter frustration, she could tell from James's expression that he was unconvinced and impatient with her efforts to explain her innocence. He gestured abruptly.

"Jane, it just doesn't matter."

"But it *does* matter to me! It matters a lot—" She had to break off and wait while they were served the first course, steaming cups of fish chowder that smelled heavenly. Hardly realizing what she was doing, Jane picked up a spoon and took a taste. "It's very good," she said miserably, and looked up, expecting to find herself still under James's cynical gaze, but he was busy eating his chowder.

"Yes . . . it is good. All the signs were right, at least so far, hmm?" He looked up and smiled soothingly, his eyes reiterating the same assurance he had just spoken: *I don't believe you, but it doesn't matter.*

Well, it mattered to Jane, who had no intention of ceasing her defense until she had convinced him, but she didn't want to argue all through the meal. She would wait until afterward. It consoled her to think that she had concrete evidence on her side. When she told James about running into Susan McGraw and showed him the key to the condominium in Florida, maybe then he would believe that she was making plans for a future that did not include tricking him into marrying her.

During the meal they avoided further controversy by keeping the conversation centered around the dishes before them, which proved to be excellent, and the topic of food in general. When they had finished the main course James quite unexpectedly—and unintentionally—gave Jane the perfect opening she needed to begin in a roundabout way another effort to convince him she wasn't involved in any scheme with Lottie, but had definite plans of her own for the future.

"How was business at the co-op this morning?" James inquired, putting down his fork and pushing back his plate that little portion of an inch that signaled he was through.

Jane unconsciously duplicated his exact motions

and sat back, eager to seize the opportunity that had been handed to her. She would have done well to organize her thoughts before beginning to speak instead of just blurting out the words as they came to mind.

"That's the exciting news I wanted to tell you about. There wasn't a single customer all morning—" She broke off with a laugh at the comical inquiry on his face. "Patience. The excitement comes later. Anyway, I had given up on seeing another soul, besides my relief, when in walked an old girlfriend I went to college with . . . Susan McGraw—I don't know whether you knew her or not." James's expression coupled with the movement of his shoulders said that the name didn't trigger any recall, and so far he hadn't gotten a glimmer of any reason for excitement either.

"It was so unexpected seeing Susan after all these years . . . pure chance that she should happen to be a guest on Islesboro and walk into the co-op today when I was there. Honestly, James, I think you'll have to agree that the whole thing was fate." Jane wasn't being intentionally dramatic, but the sudden sharpening of James's eyes made her realize he thought she was trying to build up suspense. Well, that was his problem. She would tell her own story in her own way. He could just be patient and listen.

"I won't go into all the details because you'd just be bored by them anyway, but Susan and I were very close in college, and today it seemed that all the years we hadn't seen each other just didn't matter. It was awkward for her at first because she's still rich and I'm not, but we soon got past that." Jane ignored the deepening of impatience and skepticism on James's face. He either thought she was making all this up or else slanting the account of her meeting with Susan to satisfy some devious purpose. Well, he would soon see where he was wrong.

"We were both so glad to see each other! There was so much to catch up on!" Jane's expression grew rueful. "Actually, we talked mostly about me. I told Susan about Terry . . . and the way things are with Aunt Lottie and me now. You know, James, today helped me to realize how wrong Aunt Lottie and Terry and I were to cut off all our old friends the way we did, to act as though losing all one's money is something to be ashamed of, when really it isn't."

This last, a completely impromptu digression that occurred to Jane on the spot and seemed worth sharing, was more than James could stomach in silence. He made a sound between a sigh and a groan.

"Is this insight the 'discovery' you're so 'excited' about?" he asked cynically. What he was thinking was that losing everything might not be a good reason for cutting off one's friends, but it made some people he could name more tolerant of their old "enemies."

"No, as a matter of fact, it isn't!" Jane retorted indignantly, reaching for her handbag and wrenching open the flap. Conscious of his gaze trained on her, she rummaged around for what seemed an interminable time and finally found the key. *"This* is what I'm excited about!" Jane brandished the key triumphantly. "It's the key to a condominium Susan owns in Florida."

James raised one eyebrow, obviously not all impressed. "I see. And your old friend, Susan McGraw, has offered you the use of her condominium. How generous of her, especially after all this time. Is that where you're planning to go when you leave

Islesboro? When was it you said you intended to go—August? My aunt was assuring me just today that she has no intention of leaving her cottage."

Jane stared at him, aghast. *He didn't believe her! Not a single word!* He thought the whole story of Susan and the condominium was something she'd made up. Slowly she put away the key, feeling foolish about the way she'd been holding it aloft, like some tangible evidence of her credibility.

"You can believe whatever you like, James," she said in a small, proud voice. "I'm just wasting my breath trying to talk to you." She *was* leaving Islesboro, with or without Lottie. James's failure to believe her wouldn't change that. She didn't understand why it upset her so deeply for him to have such a wrong picture of her.

"I've tried to tell you, Jane. It doesn't *matter.*" There was a curiously grim gentleness in James's voice that only deepened Jane's frustration and her despair.

She shook her head slowly. "I don't understand what you mean when you keep saying that. It *does* matter to me that you think I'm a liar."

Their waitress had started to approach the table earlier and been halted by a signal from James. Now he summoned her with a brief nod and she came to clear the table and offer them dessert and coffee.

Jane shook her head at once, not even wanting to hear the dessert choices. "No, nothing for me." Hopeless as it seemed, she still wanted to convince James somehow that she wasn't an accomplice in a plot to take advantage of him.

"Just bring our check, please," James bade the waitress. He watched Jane slip one hand up to her neck and massage the tense muscles. Suddenly he couldn't wait to get out of the restaurant and take her to his cottage, where they could be alone. Nothing that had happened today—and God knows a lot had happened—changed his need to hold Jane in his arms. He'd take her clothes off and ease away all that tension, show her with the touch of his hands and his kisses what he'd been trying to tell her: She and his aunt had waged a successful campaign and won. James was the willing conquered. It only remained to negotiate some of the terms of surrender.

"James, what exactly did you and Aunt Lottie say to each other today?" The weary persistence of Jane's tone indicated perfectly her state of mind: She was sick of this whole subject, but couldn't leave it. "And don't you *dare* tell me it doesn't matter."

James saw the waitress coming with the customary little tray bearing the check. He took out his wallet, extracted an amount that would cover the total and a generous tip, and placed the bills on top of the check before the young woman could leave the tray on the table.

"Our compliments to the owners. Everything was to our satisfaction," he told the waitress pleasantly, and then rose and came around to stand behind Jane's chair, the urge to touch her at once too strong for him to suppress. His hands settled on the tense shoulder muscles and massaged lightly as he bent forward and said close to her ear, "I promise not to say that again, *ever,* if it bothers you."

He had taken Jane by surprise with his swift movement and the lightning change in mood. She sat torn by conflicting reactions to his touch and the tone of his voice. His hands felt wonderful on her body, even here in a public place. She wanted to breathe out a little sigh, relax, surrender to the comfort and the strength, but there had been that placating note beneath the seduction in his voice. He was willing to humor her if she insisted, but he still didn't believe in her innocence.

Jane did let out a sigh, but one of renewed exasperation, not of surrender. "You might as well tell me what the two of you said to each other, because I won't give up. I intend to get Aunt Lottie's version too." She made a move to rise, but James's hands closed around her shoulders briefly, keeping her in the chair, asserting the easy dominance and control beneath the indulgence of his reply. "I'll tell you every single word that passed between my aunt and me." He released her shoulders after a final caressing pressure and pulled back her chair.

A short time had elapsed between the time James rose from his chair and the two of them walked out of the restaurant, and the scene would have appeared perfectly normal to any casual observer, exciting no special interest, but to Jane it recapped the evening so far, bringing into play James's strange new proprietorial manner and the utter futility of her efforts to communicate with him. What made the situation even more intolerable for her was the inescapable fact that James's distrust in no way diminished the intense physical attraction that had simmered between them all evening and now leaped higher as James took every opportunity to touch her.

True, his attentions were all courteous. He grasped her elbows as she rose from her chair, guided her from the room with a light touch at the small of her back, seated her so solicitously in the Ferrari that she had the ridiculous feeling of having been picked up and placed inside. When he slid into the driver's seat Jane was fighting the sheer pleasure of being treated like something precious. All the places he had touched so lightly glowed with warmth, and her body ached for a more encompassing, less gentle contact.

"*James . . .*" She spoke his name as a protest against her own longings as well as against the failures of the evening.

He had fitted the key in the ignition and was about to start the engine, but her voice exploded the urgency inside him, and he acted without thought, turning toward her and sliding an arm around her shoulder. He squeezed her tight, letting her absorb the shudder that rippled through him.

"*Jane,*" he whispered with no protest whatever, just acceptance and a longing so powerful he could hardly contend with it. "Help me . . . wait." He kissed her forehead, her eyebrows, her cheeks, and then brushed his lips against hers before drawing back with a harshly indrawn breath. "It will be different for us both this time, my darling." His eyes held hers as he brought his free hand up to her face and made a tender stroking motion before he drew it away and took his arm from around her.

As Jane looked into his eyes she had the panicky feeling that she was being sucked beyond her depth. The possessiveness was out in the open now, having grown by leaps and bounds along with the burgeoning of his passion. The two emotions together formed a fierce mixture that evidently brought him as much torment as pleasure, as much self-contempt as triumph. Tearing her gaze free of his, Jane realized her panic had deepened into fear. She had to fight him! Somehow she had to resist the powerful pull he was exerting over her with the very force of his personality and will.

"James, you promised we would have a meal and talk—nothing else," she reminded desperately as he pulled away from the curb.

His quick, frowning glance held rebuke. "I thought we'd gotten past the stage where you feel obligated to resist."

It was the disappointment more than the scorn that bothered her. He thought her reservation about giving herself to him again sexually was just another brand of dishonesty.

"James, I can't win with you, no matter what I say, no matter what I *do!*" she cried out in sheer exasperation.

"Actually just the opposite is true, Jane," he contradicted her tersely. "You can't lose."

Further conversation seemed pointless since everything she said was turned against her. A sense of helplessness swept her as the Ferrari quickly ate up the scant distance between the village and the turnoff to James's cottage. When James braked and turned, she lacked the strength of will to take control and order him to drive her home instead. James had taken over. All evening she had battered herself against his certitude and only bruised herself in the process. For the time being she didn't have the heart to fight him.

The defeated quality in Jane's capitulation bothered James, perhaps because as long as she kept protesting, he'd held out that glimmer of hope that perhaps she *was* being honest with him. But, as he'd been telling her all evening, it didn't matter. He wanted her. That was the central fact of his existence he was admitting once again, at the cost of his pride. To have her at long last would be supplying the missing ingredient in his life.

There was no denying the tang of bitterness in the cup of victory from which he was finally going to drink, but better the aftertaste than the alternative thirst. To have Jane "settle" for him as a solution to her and Lottie's financial predicament rankled like hell, but he still needed her in his life the way a plant needed sunshine. The analogy wasn't an accidental one. James supposed he had always equated Jane's warmth and generosity and "goodness" with the generative powers of the sun's rays but also with its gifts of simple pleasure. He intended to bask in those pleasures at considerable cost and take the full risk of exposure.

These reflections brought a grim satisfaction to James's breast and helped him to subdue the overwhelming immediacy of his passion. By the time he had parked the Ferrari and taken Jane inside the house, his mind was in control of the needs of his body. It wouldn't do for him to grab her the way he had in the car and carry on like a sex-crazed adolescent. Tonight he intended to drive her crazy before he satisfied her. He wanted her to beg him to make love to her and wipe out, once and for all, any pretence of reluctance.

He had a fire laid in the fireplace of the library, where Jane had surprised him several days ago. She was secretly relieved that whatever was going to happen between them tonight wouldn't be taking place in the living room. It had already become haunted for her, peopled with her own ghost and James's acting out a scene that would intrude painfully upon the present.

James looked up from his kneeling position at the hearth, where he was touching a match to wadded newspaper and kindling. The abstracted expression on her face brought a mixture of curiosity and jealousy to his breast. She looked a million miles away from him. His first instinct was to bring her back.

"What are you thinking?" he asked abruptly and watched her closely, noting the quick defensiveness.

Like so many reflections that seem crystal-clear in the conception, this one wasn't easy to verbalize, but Jane found that she wanted to share the thought with him. "Oh, that you and I tend to leave our mark upon a place once we've been there together." From the comprehension in James's eyes she thought she needn't belabor the point; he seemed to have understood immediately.

Jane smiled as she glanced around the rather somber room with its dark leather furniture and book-lined walls. "After tonight this room will be haunted, too, I suppose. Years from now when I'm old and gray, perhaps I'll come to the door and ask the owners if they would be so kind as to let me look around. Who knows? Maybe you'll even come back here someday and visit the scene of your youthful 'storm and stress.'" Jane cleared her throat self-consciously. Beneath the whimsy of her projection into the future had crept an unexpected sadness that was partly regret for the relationship she and James would never have together and partly a premature nostalgia.

"This room is already haunted," James stated quietly, rising to his feet with that fluid grace of movement Jane had always admired. "And I don't have to go through with selling this place, you know, not if you want me to keep it. You could leave your 'mark' on every square inch of it."

Jane was grappling with the first remark and coming up with a blank. "But I was only in this room once before that I can remember. . . ." That had been the day James was taking books off the shelves. Nothing had really happened between them. "And whether you keep this place or sell it has nothing whatever to do with me. I won't be here."

"Oh, but it has everything to do with you," he contradicted her softly.

Jane watched him coming toward her and her heartbeat quickened at the seductive promise that gleamed in his eyes.

"James—" she warned him half-heartedly, knowing full well that she wanted him to take her into his arms, hold her close, and kiss her.

"Jane—" he mocked her softly, stopping in front of her and bringing his hands up to frame her face so lightly that she could easily have jerked away. "Don't worry . . . I'm only going to do *this*. . . ." He brought his lips to hers, but then he didn't actually kiss her at all. He just brushed his mouth along the full, sensuous shape of hers and stroked her bottom lip with the tip of his tongue.

Jane felt her head tilting back and her mouth softening and parting. She was trying to keep her hands from slipping up to grasp the back of his head when he dropped his away from her face and stepped back.

"Come and sit by the fire," he invited her. "Would you like a brandy or a coffee?"

She blinked at him, disgruntled. "Neither, thanks."

He left her to walk over to a bar concealed behind cabinet doors. "Something else then? Wine, champagne?" he inquired while he poured himself a brandy.

"Nothing," Jane refused shortly and marched around the sofa to sit down in an armchair. He could have the sofa all to himself with his brandy.

But James didn't sit on the sofa. Without any comment on her choice of seats or even a raised eyebrow to suggest she was acting out of a spirit of pique, he sat down at her feet. Setting the snifter of brandy safely to one side, he slipped off his shoes and tossed them away. Then he leaned back, one shoulder resting solidly against her knee.

"Now, isn't this peaceful and domestic?" he inquired blandly, twisting around and glancing up at her.

Jane glared down at him. "Peaceful and domestic," she agreed sarcastically. "You surprise me, James. I didn't know you were the domestic type."

The words were no sooner out than she felt James's hand sliding up the inside of one calf, taking a turn at the knee and continuing higher. He was watching her expression as he stroked upward along the inside of her thigh.

"I never have been, but I might get to like it," he murmured. "You're so soft here. Your skin is like warm satin." His fingertips reached an elastic barrier that failed to keep out the warm tingles of sensation he was arousing with his unhurried caresses. Then without warning he idly brushed the silken inset of her panties, back and forth, the friction creating a heat that burned into her.

Jane felt her thighs relaxing apart in response to the

reflexive surge that shot through her. When his fingers eased beneath the elastic, she knew he would find a telltale moistness. Her face must be mirroring for his satisfaction the sensual expectation he was building up in her as she waited, but she couldn't bring herself to stop him. And then the deep probe of a finger found the live ache inside her and focused all her attention upon the intolerable pleasure of the invasion. Moaning softly, she leaned her head back against the chair cushion and slid a little deeper, opening her legs wider to him.

Her total surrender aroused him as much as the tactile stimulus of delving into the hot velvet wetness. As he slowly withdrew his hand from between her thighs, James had to concentrate hard on subduing the great surge in his loins that made him want to pull her down on the floor and cover her body with his in the most elemental kind of mating ritual.

"Come down here with me," he ordered softly, taking her by the waist but applying little actual force as she came willingly. "I want to make you feel wonderful everywhere." He was already sliding down the zipper of her skirt.

Jane made several attempts to help him undress her, but he checked her each time, enforcing his own unhurried pace and stopping to pay homage to each newly exposed portion of bare flesh. As he unclipped the front clasp of her bra and pulled the lace cups free of her breasts, he bent and kissed each dusky peak and nuzzled the full curves with his lips.

"I remember the year these bloomed practically overnight," he mused.

"Do you remember embarrassing the very life out of me?" There was too much passion in Jane's voice to leave much room for indignation. James's low chuckle, followed by the raspy warmth of his tongue, contracted her already hard nipples into tighter knots.

He lifted his head and grinned down at her, sharing a reminiscence that for once wasn't painful. "You have to look at it from my point of view. The summer before you had been flat as a board. And then there you were sporting these beauties." He cupped her breasts, looking down at them, caressing them with the admiration in his eyes. "I'd spent the past nine months off at school with a bunch of guys who thought about and talked of little besides the anatomy of girls."

"I'll never forget that day I walked out in my new bathing suit, self-conscious as all get-out anyway, and you let out a wolf whistle and called out, 'Hey—'"

"—look at the knockers on Jane," James chimed in and then threw back his head and laughed. When Jane pushed him in mock reproof, he fell back on the floor without a struggle, smiling up at her. "What you didn't realize then was that I was cleaning up my language," he teased. "The word in my mind at the time wasn't *knockers.*"

"All I know is that I wanted to fall into a crack and hide," Jane scolded him, crouching beside him on her knees, unembarrassed at being bare-breasted. She set about very efficiently unbuttoning his shirt and pulling it free of his trousers so that she could enjoy the view of his chest and hard, flat stomach at the same time that she explored them with her palms.

James's brain sent out a warning that things were not proceeding according to his plan, but Jane was already bending lower, brushing her lips across his taut brown skin, finding the tiny nipples and worrying them with her tongue. He heard the weakness of his voice as he murmured her name, and thought he knew how Samson must have felt in Delilah's power.

"James, I love your body." She unbuckled his belt and undid the fastening to his trousers before he could muster either the will or the strength to stop her. Then she lay next to him and brought her lips to his in a kiss that distracted him from her intention until he felt her hand slide down his belly, inside the trousers. As she gently closed her fingers around his swollen hardness, he couldn't keep back the groan of exquisite pleasure.

"Yes," he whispered against her lips as she released him and then worked her fingertips tentatively underneath the elastic waistband of his briefs. When she captured his tumescence in her bare hand, James lay back, awash on a wave of sensation that curved higher and higher as she squeezed gently. "Easy," he warned in a pained voice, and then was sorry when her hand withdrew.

She had paused to finish undressing him and herself. There was almost enough time for James to collect himself and get back on course with his plan to torment her at some length before he actually made love to her. But when she lay next to him and asked simply, "Will you make love to me, James—now?" it was not in his power to refuse her. There was nothing he wanted more in the world than to please her in the way that he knew he could.

This time he held her in his arms afterward. Jane nestled close, as devastated by the tumult of their lovemaking as she had been the night before, but aware that there had been a difference, a kind of fierce tenderness that had been missing last night. With her mind not entirely clear, she reasoned fuzzily that once past that first time there wasn't the matter of concession, of giving in. Instead, there was mutual giving and taking.

"James, you are a wonderful lover," she said softly as he stirred, and she sensed that he would be drawing away. "I wonder if there's another man in the world who can make me feel the way you do." To her surprise, the honest sentiment must not have pleased him, because his withdrawal was immediate. He slid his arm from under her and sat up.

"What's wrong?" Jane asked in a perplexed voice, pushing up on her elbows and searching his face. Was this going to be a replay of the previous night? "Does it bother you for me to tell you I think you're a good lover? After what just happened, you can't doubt that I'm sincere."

James rose and went over to tend to the fire. As she watched him, Jane was tempted to utter another honest compliment. He was magnificent as he leaned forward from the waist and jabbed at the fire with the poker, the lines of his body sinuous and graceful, the muscles taut and yet smooth. To look at him gave her pleasure.

As he returned the poker to the stand and straightened, James was intensely aware of her gaze and turned to meet it. The thrill of possession he'd been feeling all afternoon rose up inside him as he looked at her, naked and yet completely natural and unashamed to be so in front of him. *She was his*. That was all that really mattered.

"No man minds being told he's a good lover. But he

doesn't like to know that the woman he's going to marry is wondering if some other man could please her better." James had expected some show of surprise at his mention of marriage, but Jane looked as though lightning had struck. James didn't think she was that good an actress. Was it possible he had wronged her and she *wasn't* in league with his aunt, as she had been insisting all along?

Jane sat up and looked around abstractedly for her clothes. What had unnerved her even more than James's oblique announcement of his intentions was her own totally unexpected reaction to it. There had been a wild lurch in her breast, followed by a flood of sweetness that quickly dried up at the hardness in James's face. He wasn't looking at her the way a man looks at a woman he wants to marry, with tenderness and love. *Fool!* Jane denounced herself as she got up from the floor and began dressing, her heart like a lump of lead inside her. Until this moment she would have sworn she harbored no hope of a future with James. Her disappointment was evidence that she had.

"It was a stupid thing to say. I didn't mean to bruise your male ego. But then, I didn't know I was the woman you intended to marry, either. You hadn't consulted me on the matter." She felt incredibly clumsy and uncoordinated under his narrow gaze. The two parts of the clasp of her bra no longer fit together, the buttonholes of her blouse weren't large enough for the buttons now, and the zipper of her skirt stuck twice.

James wanted to go over and help her, but he needed to keep his distance until everything had been said. Since she was taking so long, he might as well get dressed himself, he thought, although it was silly. They would both only be taking the clothes off again. He meant for her to stay the night with him . . . *every* night from now on. That had such irresistible allure, he was able to push aside his repugnance for the conditions under which he would finally possess her.

Chapter Eight

$\mathcal{T}$ension never interfered with James's coordination or dexterity. He was dressed and waiting for Jane's attention when she sat back down in the same chair she had previously occupied and pushed her feet into her shoes.

"Now can we talk?" He was eager to get the thing over with. It had all been settled in his mind since that afternoon.

Jane realized she had been procrastinating, fumbling around like a two-year-old just learning to dress herself, because she dreaded what was coming.

"James, I've been trying to talk to you all night, but you refused to listen to me. I know you have some notion in your head that I'm on the bargaining block and available to the highest bidder, but that's *not true*." She watched him shrug his shoulders impatiently and knew that once again he didn't believe her.

"That key I showed you tonight really fits the door of a condominium in Florida, where I intend to live when I leave Islesboro—until I can afford a place of my own. I'm really going, James. In fact . . ." The thought must have been there inside her head since lunch, and now it emerged. "Susan said I could go there anytime. There's no real reason to wait—" She broke off in response to the sound James made.

"You're not going off to any condominium in Florida, Jane, and we both know it. How the hell would you make it on your own? You've never held a job in your life or made a decision that counted." He held up a hand to check her when she opened her mouth to contradict him. "Wait—hear me out. You may have *thought* the decision to marry my cousin was your own, but it wasn't. It was my aunt's. She had been programming you to do her bidding since you were ten." James's voice had gentled on those last words out of pity for Jane, who had shrunk back into her chair, her face pale and taut. Even though he hadn't finished all he intended to say, he paused and let silence fill the room while she summoned her defenses. He hadn't expected the truth to hit her so hard.

Jane rose from her chair and walked around behind the sofa, where she stood with straight shoulders, her fingertips just barely touching the supple leather of the top of the sturdy sofa she had put between them. Slowly she shook her head. "You certainly have a high opinion of me, don't you, James? Why on earth would you agree to marry such a 'pathetic' individual, anyway? What could I possibly offer a man like you who has everything?" She held up both hands and warded him off with her palms as he made a movement and started to speak. "No, *you* wait now and let me have *my* say.

"No matter what you choose to believe, I married Terry because I wanted to. I loved him, and he loved me. Aunt Lottie may have favored the match, but she couldn't have forced either of us to feel the way we felt toward each other. So you're wrong, James. I *have* made at least one important decision in my life." Jane's eyes held his unwaveringly. If she had wanted to be cruel, she could have pointed out that she had made *two* crucial life decisions simultaneously: to marry Terry and *not* to marry James, but it wasn't necessary to say it aloud. The fact hung there between them.

James jammed his hands down into his trouser pockets and widened his stance. "So I was wrong," he stated tersely, without any expression. "You have made a decision. Are you going to tell me now that I'm also mistaken in suggesting that you are une-quipped to go out into the world and support your-self? What kind of job training have you had? What kind of work do you intend to do when you get to Florida? It's easy to sit here on Islesboro and day-dream about a life of financial independence in a balmy climate, Jane, but the reality is going to be something quite different." He sighed impatiently. Pulling his right hand out of his pocket, he half-turned toward the fireplace and rested his elbow on the mantel. "Look—"

"I know it's not going to be easy for me," Jane broke in quickly before he could say more. She didn't want James to make the offer that she would be compelled to refuse. "But it's more than a daydream, James. I'm leaving Islesboro . . . very soon, maybe in only a week or two, and *without* Aunt Lottie if she sticks by what she told you and won't leave with me. I have a place to stay and enough money saved to keep me going a couple of months, anyway." The skepticism in James's face made her speak faster. She simply *had* to convince him.

"This spring I've been keeping aside the money I earned from my needlework. You forget that I know how much things cost. After all, I've been buying the food and paying the bills for six years now. And there's no reason I can't earn enough money to support myself. I may not have any specialized job skills, but I can check out groceries in a supermarket or wait tables or clerk in a store or do *something* while I take night classes and learn whatever I need to know to get a better job. After all, I'm not stupid." She smiled wryly. "I wish I were as confident as I sound. Actually, I *am* a little scared, James, at the thought of being completely on my own . . . but I'm excited too." Her eyes shyly begged his understanding.

James felt a steel band tightening around his chest. He took a deep breath to try to loosen it. "If you want to get a job and prove that you can earn your own money, that's fine with me, Jane. I have no objection to a wife with a career. I'll even back you in a business venture of your own if you find something that appeals to you." She was standing as still as a statue, as though the act of listening required everything of her. James hadn't an inkling of her thoughts.

"What I'm saying is that you can call the shots on everything with one exception. You can work or not work, as you please. We can live anywhere you choose. I can conduct my business from anywhere on the globe where there's an airport and a telephone.

I'll see that my aunt is well taken care of. If she insists upon staying here on Islesboro, I'll have her cottage restored and hire a housekeeper-companion to look out for her. There's only one thing I *won't* agree to ever and I want that understood: My aunt will not live with us or even be invited for long visits. She's no longer to have any control over what you do or what you think." James had braced himself to deal with any show of resistance, but, to his relief, there was none, just sadness and regret, feelings he was sure she would get over in time once she'd made the break with his aunt and plunged into a new life.

Jane wished desperately that somehow she had prevented James from issuing his proposal, which, like the first one some six years ago, hadn't made any mention of that most important reason that two people would marry: love. To turn him down now would hurt as it hadn't before because Jane hadn't cared for James then . . . *and she did now*. He had permitted her to look beneath his defenses and discover a man of sensitivity whom she found most compelling. But to marry him now, under the circumstances, was out of the question. She was afraid that he would never understand that.

"James, I'm sorry, but I couldn't marry *anyone* right now," Jane said gently, coming from behind the sofa and taking a few steps toward him. "Maybe you were more accurate a few minutes ago than I was willing to admit. I can't deny that Aunt Lottie has been a powerful influence in my life. She was so good to me that I always wanted to please her as a kind of repayment." Jane winced in advance of the unpalatable admission she felt compelled to make next. "Maybe the desire for her approval even affected my decision to marry Terry, but I had decided that long before she lost everything. I couldn't possibly have backed out and still lived with myself." She made a restless movement. "But that's all done now and in the past. It's the present that matters. I don't want to be taken care of by you or Aunt Lottie or anybody else, and I don't want *anyone* telling me what to do or think. I want to stand on my own two feet and live my own life." Her expression turned pleading. "I've been trying to tell you that, James, and you refused to believe me. But please don't hate me for turning you down."

James stared at her unbelievingly. "I know what you've been telling me," he muttered. "You've been telling me *this*—" He moved so fast, Jane was taken completely off guard. Before she could guess his intentions, he had caught her close to him and was kissing her hard, with anger and passion and a kind of desperation.

When Jane didn't struggle, but didn't respond, either, he held her even tighter and deepened the intensity of the kiss, plunging his tongue into her mouth and finding hers, forcing it to couple with his until with a little moan Jane finally responded. When her hands slid up around his neck and she began kissing him back, James no longer had to hold her to keep her from trying to escape. He ran his hands over her back and shoulders, down along her hips and buttocks, his desire for her reawakened and infused with an urgency more powerful than simple passion. He needed to possess her again to establish his claim and prove to her in a way words couldn't express that she was *his*.

"James, don't . . . don't, please don't!" Jane

stirred against him, uttering this plea as he found the zipper of her skirt and started sliding it down. Something exploded inside James. He jerked the zipper to the end of its length and let the skirt fall on the floor.

Jane went rigid at first, too surprised at what was happening to put up a fight, but when he proceeded to try to strip off her clothing with no more regard for her person than if she had been a plastic mannequin, she came to life.

"James, you *stop* this!" she cried out, twisting away and pushing against his chest. They stood eyeing each other like opponents in the boxing ring, chests heaving and bodies tense with readiness for the next aggressive move. Physically Jane was no match for him, and they both knew it. She never had been. In the past she had used words as her poison-tipped weapons, hurling them in what had always seemed at the time a futile attempt to hurt him. But Jane didn't want to hurt him now, not even when he resorted to his old bullying tactics. She still wished that somehow she could make him understand that she had to turn him down.

"James, this doesn't change anything." The sound of her voice might have been the ringing of the bell that signaled the end of the round. Jane knew at once that she was in no danger of further assault. The force of gravity was suddenly so overwhelming that her whole body seemed to slump downward, and she had to battle fiercely against an urge just to sink down on the floor and cry, for James, for herself, for all the misery and disappointment that the lives of humans hold.

"You *know* it doesn't change anything," she continued with considerable effort. "We have some kind of physical chemistry together—we have had for years, even when we couldn't speak a civil word to each other. But that's not substance enough for marriage. You don't love me now any more than you loved me the last time you asked me to marry you. From your own admission, you don't even have a very high opinion of my character. I'm a *person*, James, not a dutiful robot to be passed from one member of the Patton family to another."

When she had first begun speaking, the regret and sadness in her voice had come across as apology to James, causing him to stiffen and withdraw. The last thing he wanted from Jane was pity, for God's sake. The indignation in her final remarks came as a relief as she focused upon herself and not upon him. They also showed that she didn't begin to comprehend the way he felt about her. He considered for just a second trying to explain what he had never understood himself, and then quickly discounted the idea. How much devastation to his pride can a man risk, after all?

James walked over to the fireplace and took up his former position there. A dreadful pall of finality hung over the room as he spoke the words he felt compelled to say.

"I don't know much about the necessary 'substance' for a marriage, Jane, and, quite frankly, I doubt you have much reason to know about it either. Neither of us grew up in a normal family with a mother and father devoted to each other." His voice was cool and tinged with irony. "As far as talking of 'love,' you're right—I never have. What I have done, *twice*—" his voice sharpened into bitterness here—"is ask you to be my wife, an offer, incidentally, that I've never made to any other woman, with or without declarations of undying love. Before you make your refusal this time definite, I want to make one thing absolutely clear: *I will never ask you again.*"

The silence in the room was electric as his eyes held hers to emphasize that this was not staged dramatics. Jane opened her mouth to speak, but before she could, James cautioned her in the same somber tone. "Perhaps you should wait, give the matter some thought." His mouth tightened cynically. "Go home tonight and talk it over with my aunt before you make any snap decisions."

Jane's indrawn breath was audible. "There's no need to talk it over with her. It's my life, and I make my own decisions—but there's no use in telling you that, is there, James? You're going to have to see for yourself!"

"Does that mean your answer is no, then?" James inquired grimly. "Does it?" he pressed when she stared at him with huge eyes golden with frustration and deepest regret.

"My answer has to be no . . ." Her voice trailed off into a whisper. She turned to leave, and when she got to the door she stopped and spun around, expecting that he would be watching her. But he wasn't. He was facing the mantel and had both elbows propped on it, his head clutched in his hands. Anyone who saw him thus and didn't know the circumstances would have thought he was suffering acute physical pain.

Jane wanted terribly to go to him, to touch him with gentle, loving fingers that could ease the agony away, but she knew that she couldn't. He would only misinterpret her actions as a sign that she had changed her mind. And she hadn't changed her mind even though leaving James standing there immersed in his despair ripped her apart and created a great emotional gash inside her that was flooded with sharp longing. She couldn't go to James on his terms, not now when she didn't feel as though she were a complete person. He should have understood that she needed the opportunity to find out exactly who and what she was.

Outside, Jane realized she would have to walk home, but not for a second did she consider going back inside and asking James to drive her. Her steps were rapid as she walked along the dark lane to the highway, not from any fear of danger to her person, but because she needed to put distance between herself and the man back there at the cottage. The totally new possibility that James might *need* her threatened to erode her certainty that she was doing the right thing. She had to keep reminding herself that he hadn't had to make his marriage proposal an ultimatum. He could have given her time and space and understanding.

He would have . . . if he loved her.

But James didn't love her. That reminder helped, more than anything else, to keep her from turning back. His emotion was real and very powerful, but it wasn't—as she had told him—the "substance" upon which to build a marriage. For reasons Jane couldn't fathom, she had long ago become the prize in a competition James had set up in his own mind. Now, even after his cousin, the original imaginary competitor, was gone, James was still determined to have her. Perhaps he was trying to make amends to himself for the slights he had suffered at the hands of his aunt and her household in his youth.

Whatever the complex reasons for James's obsession with having her, Jane's own deepest instincts told her she could be hurt if she got any further involved with James than she was at this moment. Already she cared for him to the extent that it had taken all her willpower to leave him, knowing that he was hurting. She had had to struggle against the impulse to do what was best for James instead of what was best for Jane.

If she had given herself to James and satisfied that terrible longing that apparently had built up within him through the years, until now it was a kind of fixation, what then? How long would James want her? Wasn't the thrill always in the winning of the trophy and not in its actual possession? Jane shivered with the coolness of the night and walked even faster.

Lottie had already gone to bed. Jane took extreme care not to waken her because she dreaded having to endure another confrontation when mentally and emotionally she felt ripped apart. Tomorrow would be soon enough to face Lottie with the news of what had transpired between James and herself tonight, soon enough for Jane to announce an ultimatum of her own.

Jane slept fitfully and awoke early, consumed with a kind of panicky restlessness. Sitting up in bed, she pressed a hand over her heart and felt its rapid beat. *I have to go . . . now . . . today,* she found herself thinking and then tried to banish the urgency. She needn't be in that big a hurry. She had given herself until the end of August, hadn't she?

As she got out of bed Jane faced the truth head-on. She didn't trust herself to wait that long and not have her resolve worn down by a coalition between James and Lottie. It might be cowardice on her part, but she was going to obey her instinct to flee.

Departing from her usual morning ritual, she did not go directly to the kitchen to brew herself a pot of tea and prepare a second pot so that she had only to heat the water when Lottie arose. Instead, she quickly made her bed and began to take clothes out of bureau drawers and stack them into neat piles. Next, she went through her clothes hanging in the closet, selecting those that she would take with her.

In a surprisingly short time she was finished. Now she was ready to get her luggage from an upstairs storage room, where it had rested, unused, for six years. The white leather was musty and darkened with mildew, but the oval gold plates with her initials in fancy script still shone, a reminder of those carefree days when she would embark upon a shopping spree to Paris or a ski holiday in Switzerland with a half dozen pieces of luggage.

So much had happened since then that Jane was an entirely different person now. She had the odd feeling that she might be borrowing an old friend's luggage as she picked out several pieces and carried them downstairs. The door of her bedroom stood open, as she had left it, but everything was not the same inside. Lottie stood at the end of her bed, attired in dressing gown and slippers, staring at the neat piles of clothes. Her head swung around toward Jane, and her eyes narrowed to slits as they focused upon the mildewed suitcases.

"What on *earth* is going on here?" Lottie demanded.

Jane walked inside the room and set the pieces of

luggage on the floor beside the bed. How ridiculous of her to react to Lottie's accusing query with all the guilt and panic of a truant schoolchild! She was a grown woman, not a ten-year-old.

"As you can see, I'm packing, Aunt Lottie." Jane stood, her hands on her hips, looking at the suitcases. "First, though, I'm going to have to clean these," she added matter-of-factly, as though her revelation hadn't hit the other woman like a bombshell.

"Packing—what do you mean, you're *packing*—" Lottie broke off, her frown smoothing out. "Why, of course," she said archly, her face taking on a pleased expression. "Don't let me interrupt, dear. Continue with your packing."

Jane's mouth went slack with amazement. Whatever she had expected in the way of a reaction from her mother-in-law, it wasn't this! And then she had a glimmer of comprehension that explained the sudden turnabout—Lottie thought Jane was eloping with James.

"I've decided to leave immediately instead of waiting until summer is over. The sooner I can get down to Florida and settled, the sooner I can get a job." The pleased expression vanished from Lottie's face. Jane talked faster as disbelief in the older woman's eyes was joined by icy rage. "You're welcome to come with me now, if you want, Aunt Lottie—or you can join me later, if this is too quick for you. But you might as well know that I've made up my mind to go. Now, I'd better see about cleaning up these suitcases."

"Well! Of all the—the *ungrateful . . . selfish*—" Lottie stammered out until, words failing her, she had to content herself with glaring her accusation. Her head was thrown back in the old imperious gesture,

but her face was mottled with helpless fury. "What happened last night?" she hissed when she was able to speak at all. "What did you do to spoil things with James? I thought—"

Jane had turned pale under the venom in her mother-in-law's voice. She felt as though she had been spewed with acid that burned right through her skin to her vital parts inside, destroying something that could never be resurrected.

"I know what you thought, Aunt Lottie," she said grimly. "You and James both thought you could run my life without any interference from me, but you're wrong, you see. I intend to live my own life from now on, make my own decisions." As she turned away, Jane was shaking inside. More than anything else, she wished she could wipe out the mental vision of the older woman's face the way it had turned ugly with outrage and contempt. Jane would never have believed Lottie could harbor such feelings toward her if they hadn't come to the surface so visibly as not to be denied. This was the woman to whom she had given her love and loyalty.

"Jane, honey, I'm sorry—please forgive me—"

The low, imploring words came from just behind Jane. She hunched a little forward in resistance, but when Lottie touched her, she turned around with an anguished cry. "Oh, Aunt Lottie!" They clung to each other, the tears running down their faces, but the sick feeling inside Jane didn't go away. She knew the relationship between herself and Lottie would never be the same after this. Lottie had killed something that could never be rekindled, perhaps childhood trust.

"It's okay, Aunt Lottie. It's okay," Jane said, her throat full of tears.

"I've always wanted what's best for you, Jane," Lottie said sorrowfully. "James would make you a good husband. You wouldn't lack for anything."

Jane pulled gently away, appalled at herself for the cynicism of the thought that came instantly to mind: *Neither would* YOU *lack for anything, Aunt Lottie.* Not wanting to broaden the rupture between Lottie and herself that was already there, Jane didn't speak the thought aloud, but one equally as true.

"James might make me a good husband, but I'm afraid I wouldn't make him a very good wife, not at this point," she said firmly. "I convinced James of that fact last night." Jane would have been well within her rights if she had rebuked Lottie for leading James into thinking Jane was willing to marry him for a price, but Lottie looked like a shipwreck victim who'd just seen a life ring float out of reach. Jane didn't have the heart to make her feel worse.

"Now I'd better get these suitcases cleaned up and finish my packing," she said briskly, declaring the whole case closed.

"You aren't planning to leave today?"

The naked desperation in Lottie's voice clutched at Jane. The ugly scene that had just transpired didn't keep her from empathizing with the other woman's situation. She thought of how terrifying it must be for Lottie to think of being all alone here at the cottage.

"Why don't you come with me, Aunt Lottie?" she urged impulsively. "We could begin a whole new life together. It'd be good for you to get away from here."

Lottie stiffened in immediate resistance. "I can't

just go away and leave . . . *everything,*" she said accusingly. "Why, it would take weeks, months, to close up the house. I suppose you mean to take the car, leave me without any transportation whatever. Well, I won't hear of it. That car belongs to me. I never thought to see this day—" She swept out of the room, her shoulders erect and her head thrown back.

Jane stood there a moment, a victim of her own mixed emotions. She was as relieved as she was disappointed by Lottie's reaction, and flooded with guilt at the thought that she might have *wanted* to leave her alone. No, she had been perfectly sincere in her offer! Lottie was making her own choice and being needlessly petty in her refusal to let Jane take the old car, which had minimal resale value and was of no other use to Lottie, since she couldn't drive it herself.

Jane considered going after Lottie and settling the issue of the car at once, but then she decided it would be best for both of them if Jane finished her packing and gave Lottie some time to think. When the older woman saw that Jane was firm in her intention to leave, she would give in. Whatever Lottie's faults, she had never been an ungenerous woman with her material possessions.

James was carrying his suitcases down the stairs when the phone rang, splintering the silence in the old cottage. At the bottom of the stairs he put the suitcases down and stood, undecided, staring at the telephone on the hall table. Its old-fashioned design was very popular these days, but this one was an original. Should he answer it or just get in his car and drive off? His judgment weighed heavily toward the latter, but he found himself picking up the receiver.

"Hello." At the first sound of his aunt's voice he cursed himself mentally for being a fool, but she elicited his complete attention at once.

"James, you have to *do* something quickly. Jane is packing to leave this very moment. She has some fool notion of going to Florida and getting a job. James, what am I going to do?" The desperation was unfeigned. "If only we could manage to stop her until we could talk some sense into her head! I have refused to let her take the car, but I couldn't physically prevent her! James, you must help me—"

"Calm down," James ordered soothingly, his mind working fast. He didn't doubt that his aunt was telling him the truth: Jane was packing with the intention of leaving Islesboro immediately, this very day. There could be only one explanation for such a hurried departure. She didn't trust herself to stay longer. The resolve to leave was based on a shaky foundation.

James was stirred with a reluctant admiration for his aunt. She had sized up the situation and hit upon the most logical obstacle they might throw into Jane's path. It would be incredibly easy to delay Jane's flight from Islesboro. James could slip over there and put the car out of commission without Jane being any the wiser.

"James, what shall I *do?*"

The faintly aggrieved note beneath Lottie's desperation brought James to his senses. Dear God, how could he even fleetingly entertain the thought of conspiring with Lottie against Jane, who was like a long-confined bird fluttering her wings against the sides of the cage. He was full of trepidations about her ability to survive in the wild, but he had to do whatever he could to set her free.

"Let her take the car. She has every right to it. And give her whatever money you have in the bank too."

There was a silence. He could feel the waves of resistance as Lottie instinctively rejected what he was ordering her to do, but her rapid capitulation came as no surprise. James knew his aunt was a self-centered woman, but not stupid. *He* was her lifeline, not Jane.

"Whatever you say, James."

It wasn't necessary for them to verbalize the bargain that had been struck. Lottie would obey James's wishes and let Jane go, but in return he would see to Lottie's needs. What she didn't know and he would never tell her was that she wasn't gaining anything he hadn't already decided to give her. There would never be any affection between himself and his aunt, but he couldn't sit by and know that she was in need when he easily had the means to help her.

He had assumed he would be providing for Jane, too, since he hadn't really believed she would actually desert Lottie. Even now, as he did his part in helping Jane make her flight south, he didn't think she would survive on her own. The odds had it that she would be back, seeking the safety of the cage.

"James, one more thing." The conspiratorial tone curdled James's blood. "Shall I tell Jane that you and I, er, *spoke* about this matter?"

James ground his teeth together, but he managed to sound as if he merely found Lottie's question absurd. "I can't think of any reason why not. You can tell her I wish her all the luck in the world." The brisk finality in his tone should set things straight with Lottie.

James had meant it last night when he told Jane he wouldn't ask her to marry him again. No matter what happened in the future, James intended to keep that promise.

Lottie Patton hung up the phone, a much relieved woman. In her own mind she had rescued Jane's future as well as her own. Lucky for that foolish girl that James was apparently willing to indulge this brainstorm of hers about running off to Florida. It shouldn't take long for her to realize she'd made a dreadful mistake. She'd be back, fully repentant and ready to recognize the wisdom of marrying a man who could take care of her.

For a moment the reality of Jane's leaving, even temporarily, brought a shaft of bleakness that sent Lottie searching immediately for her deck of cards. She wouldn't think about the being alone. She wouldn't think about anything. It was enough to know that she would be able to stay here in this place that held so many memories of her dearest Terence. That's all she asked, really, was to stay and drift from day to day in the sameness. Why couldn't Jane understand that and humor her?

As she finished packing, Jane realized that the discomfort in her insides was attributable to more than just nerves. Her stomach was protesting the break with morning custom. Jane hadn't had her usual pot of hot tea.

In the kitchen she put on the kettle and prepared a tray with two cups, since it was clear from a glance that Lottie hadn't made herself tea either. The normalcy of the little routine was soothing. It was difficult for Jane to believe she wouldn't be here in this kitchen measuring tea into this same familiar porcelain teapot tomorrow and the next day and the next. If she allowed her mind to linger on the thought of Lottie, alone, with no one to prepare her morning tea or her meals, no one to look out after her, Jane knew she wouldn't be able to go, and she had to, since staying wouldn't actually solve any of the problems. Her presence merely served as a buffer between Lottie and reality.

Lottie would have to face up to that reality now. She would have to recognize the need to sell the summer estate and make a new life on a more modest scale. What Jane wasn't reckoning with was James's interference.

To her relief Lottie apparently had accepted the fact of Jane's leaving. Not only was the older woman willing for Jane to take the old Lincoln, she commanded Jane to write out a check for whatever was in the bank and take that with her too. At first, Jane suspected a ploy.

"Don't be silly, Aunt Lottie!" she chided her mother-in-law. "I can't take your money. What will you live on?"

"Don't worry about me. Fortunately I have a nephew who will see that I don't lack for anything." The martyrlike tone implied that it was lucky for her she didn't have to depend on Jane, who was shirking her obligations.

"You're fooling yourself, Aunt Lottie," Jane came back sharply. "You won't get a red cent from James. He doesn't care if you starve to death." Jane started to say more to try to convince the other woman that she was clinging to a totally illusory hope, but then she abruptly changed her mind. It was futile trying to reason with Lottie. "No, Aunt Lottie, you keep the money in the bank. You'll need it. I can manage on what I have."

The two women had been having their tea in Lottie's bedroom, where Jane had found the older woman, sitting in one of the wing chairs in front of the fireplace, playing solitaire. Now Jane got up, facing the moment of actually telling Lottie good-bye before she put her luggage in the old Lincoln and drove off.

"Don't be silly. Do as I say and take the money." Lottie put down the deck of cards but was careful not to disturb the solitaire game in progress. "I'm only doing as James instructed me. I talked to him just minutes ago on the telephone." She moved the small table in front of her forward and stood up. "Jane, child, do you really have to go through with this madness?"

Jane's throat clamped closed. This Lottie speaking now and looking at her with worried eyes was the surrogate mother Jane loved. She had been gone the past year, buried in her own private grief.

"It's not madness, dear," Jane managed to get out in spite of the constriction of her throat muscles. "I hope you'll realize that soon and come to live with me in Florida. There's still plenty of time for you to change your mind and come now. We could notify Ted Blockett to put the cottage up for sale. I'm sure he would look after things here."

Lottie's answer was written plainly across her face. "I am not selling this cottage, Jane, *ever*. You might as well accept that fact. It's all I have left. There are too many memories here . . . wonderful memories as well as sad ones. If I lose this house, I would not want to live at all." Lottie held her arms out to Jane. "You go off to Florida if you must. I suppose you deserve a chance to do something foolish for a change. You were always such a good child."

Jane went into Lottie's arms, feeling ten years old again, loved, indulged. Lottie patted her back and kept on talking. "You're lucky that James is a patient man, but don't try his patience too long. He has waited a long time for what he wants, but he won't wait forever."

Jane drew away, twenty-six years old again and about to be on her own for the first time. "Aunt Lottie, exactly what did James tell you on the telephone?" Lottie recounted the conversation. Just as Jane had suspected, all the business about James waiting patiently in the wings was of Lottie's own invention, the result of wishful thinking. It did sound as though James had made some financial commitment though. Jane felt now that she could take the extra money Lottie offered.

There was a sense of anticlimax as Jane climbed into the old Lincoln and drove away. She hadn't expected the leavetaking to be made this simple for her. James had made it easy, and she felt as much resentment as gratitude toward him for his interference. Hadn't she wanted her departure to be wrenching and painful, but final? This way Lottie had still to be convinced that Jane wasn't off on a foolish adventure, but was embarking upon a new, independent life.

James and Lottie both had to be convinced of that fact. Only time would prove them wrong in their low estimation of her abilities to get along in the world. Now more than ever before, Jane was determined to succeed on her own, exhilarated at venturing out into the unknown, and . . . scared to death.

Chapter Nine

*J*ane took her small stack of mail out to the balcony. She opened Lottie's letter first, read it through quickly and then again more slowly, fighting a wave of loneliness that was mixed with other emotions. She wouldn't be human if she didn't feel some slight hurt that Lottie apparently was getting along very well without her. And yet Jane certainly wouldn't want Lottie to not be doing well.

The live-in housekeeper was working out to Lottie's satisfaction, even though she had had to do quite a bit in the way of training at first. Lottie mentioned several areas of duty that Jane suspected *she* probably hadn't excelled in either. Abe Johnson was supplying Lottie with firewood for the fireplaces again this winter, a backup source of heat since the furnace had been completely overhauled and the danger of its malfunctioning was no longer such a constant worry.

Lottie kept her big news until last. A prominent art critic from Boston had contacted her and asked to see Terry's paintings. Naturally she had agreed. He would be coming to Islesboro the following weekend and staying at the Islesboro Inn, which would be open for only a short time longer, since it was now near the end of September.

The closing of the letter was routinely affectionate, but this time Lottie did not suggest, as she had in her other letters, that Jane admit she had behaved rashly in running off to Florida and come home, where she belonged.

Jane refolded the letter, stuffed it back into its envelope, and then gazed out at the Atlantic Ocean, automatically making the comparison between this magnificent vista and the one of Penobscot Bay she had been used to looking at for the past six years. Perhaps it was fitting that this new view was larger and a little frightening at times, especially when the sky would darken and the breakers would come rumbling in and crash against the sea wall.

By contrast, the bay, as she remembered it, had been so much smaller, calmer, safer. To counteract the attacks of nostalgia, Jane had to remind herself that her life on the bank of Penobscot Bay had also been all of those things, smaller, calmer, and safer, but stultifying as well. If the Atlantic Ocean overwhelmed her sometimes with its power and vastness, it also thrilled her to the depths of her soul and infused within her a sense of her own capacity for striving and accomplishment.

Of course, it was sheer luck that she had such a view from her own private balcony, sheer luck that Susan's condominium was perfect for Jane's needs, not so large that she felt lost in it alone and furnished in an informal, comfortable style altogether suitable for the area. Jane had fallen in love with the place at once and known that she would be sorry to leave it when she had gotten a job and could see what she would be able to afford in an apartment of her own.

Finding a job had taken her almost three weeks. She had just begun to feel discouraged, but then afterward it seemed that everything had worked out perfectly. The job was exactly what Jane had been hoping to find.

She had gone to a nearby shopping mall to put in an application at a large department store just in case an opening should occur. Walking through the mall, she had passed a small crafts shop, stopped, and gone back to look inside. It featured quite a large section of needlework kits and supplies, but there were no samples on display and the arrangement was anything but eye-catching. Business apparently was slow since there were no other customers in the shop at the time and only one salesperson, a bored-looking young man who lounged behind the counter some minutes before he finally asked Jane if she wanted something special.

Speaking impulsively before she could lose her nerve, she replied briskly, "No, but I would like to see the manager, please."

Miracle of miracles, the young man didn't challenge her request. The manager, who was also the owner, was there, in the back office, buried in paperwork. He welcomed Jane with a wary courtesy.

Inwardly amazed that the person speaking was really herself, Jane introduced herself and explained that she had been looking for a job in precisely such a shop as this one because she intended in a few years to

open up one of her own. Her own main interest was
needlework. She was impressed with the needlework
inventory in this shop and had some ideas for promoting sales, display samples, for example, and free
workshops that would help to get people in and
involved in needlework as a hobby that not only was
very creative but useful.

Jane left the shop with several kits to work as
displays and a job, albeit one with a modest salary.
One of the conditions of the job was that Jane would
implement her ideas about promoting sales with needlework demonstrations and workshops. If there
proved to be enough interest, she could experiment
with classes of longer duration, using the shop's
premises. If her efforts indeed resulted in increased
sales of kits and needlework supplies, there would be
extra compensation for her.

Jane could tell that the manager was reserving his
judgment as to her chances for success, but at least
she had sold herself convincingly enough to be given a
chance. She didn't know until a month or so later that
he had been displeased with the work of the young
man who had taken his good time about waiting on
her that day and was intending to terminate his
employment soon. Jane saved the manager the trouble of actively seeking a replacement.

Still, to her the job was perfect. In her elation she
alternated between thinking that she was simply a
pawn to good fortune and giving herself credit for
taking matters into her own hands.

When she had been in Florida a month and a half,
Jane went up to Jacksonville on a weekend to visit her
mother. By this time she had worked for three weeks
and was feelingly increasingly confident that she could

get along on her own. She hadn't wanted to visit her mother until she felt that way.

Disappointingly, the weekend turned out to be more of a strain than a pleasure. Everyone including her mother and her mother's stepdaughters—but especially her mother's husband—treated Jane like visiting royalty. So much attention was given to ensuring her pleasure in every moment that, ironically, she couldn't relax and enjoy herself. Jane dared not paint too bleak a picture of her financial circumstances for fear that her mother would insist upon contributing money, and yet she tried to make it clear that she was simply a working woman on her own. However, the fact that she lived in a condominium on the ocean, owned by a rich friend, canceled out whatever effect she may have created with her description of her job.

On the drive back to Lauderdale she told herself that she had to be patient. In time her mother's family would come to accept her as an ordinary person and not some glamorous satellite outside their social sphere.

The visit intensified Jane's feeling of aloneness. Her new life was working out well, and yet she felt completely cut off from her past. Lottie, thanks to James's financial support, was getting along fine without her. Jane's mother had long ago built a comfortable life for herself that didn't include her real daughter, and nobody was more to blame for that than Jane herself.

"It'll just take time," Jane told herself, trying hard not to succumb to self-pity. "It'll just take time."

As much as anything else it was the need to talk to somebody that drove her to write Susan, knowing all the time that there was no telling when the letter would catch up with her. She told Susan all about getting a job and about the weekend visit to her mother. She ended with sincere thanks for the use of the condominium and the assurance that she would not take advantage of her old friend's generosity.

"Hopefully in a month I should be able to rent a small place of my own. If necessary, I can even take a roommate." And then, lest Susan think Jane was making a bid for sympathy, Jane added facetiously that perhaps she would take a *male* roommate.

After she had mailed the letter to Susan, Jane regretted that she had sent it, since it had been so revealing, but then, when there was no word from Susan, she put it out of her mind, musing that writing to Susan was like going to a therapist. She could get things off her chest and that was the end of it.

But two weeks ago, just when Jane began to feel under pressure to find another place to live, Susan had telephoned from New York, saying that Jane's letter had finally caught up with her. She demanded to know everything that was happening with Jane and seemed so genuinely interested, plying Jane with questions, that Jane had found herself eagerly recounting the details of her job and reporting that she had begun to make friends, male as well as female, and was enjoying quite an active social life compared to what she had been accustomed to the past six years.

"Speaking of friends," Susan, had put in, "I just met an old friend of yours, and a relative of sorts, too, I suppose. James Patton. I don't know how I've managed to miss out on *him* all these years."

It was clear to Jane from Susan's tone that Susan hadn't a clue that James was anything other than an "old friend" and "relative of sorts" to Jane. Actually there wasn't a single reason Susan shouldn't pursue a relationship, serious or casual, with James, but Jane bit her lip, saying nothing, because she was afraid she would sound as jealous as she felt. James and Susan? The thought of those two together wasn't at all pleasant.

"Jane, are you still there?"

Jane cleared her throat as though some obstruction had kept her from speaking. "How is James?" She tried to sound just mildly interested when actually she was burning with curiosity. Had James and Susan just accidentally run into each other—or had James remembered Susan's name and looked her up to keep tabs on Jane? The latter explanation should have had less appeal than it actually did.

"He looked fantastic to me. Ask me again soon and I should be able to tell you more, a *lot* more! I just adore that dark, brooding type, don't you?" Once again Jane found she couldn't muster a light, appropriate remark, which was all that was required. "Don't worry, darling!" Susan went on gaily. "I promise not to gobble your cousin up whole! Although he looked more than able to take care of himself, even with the likes of yours truly. By the way, he didn't look at all approving when I told him about your new liberated lifestyle. Which reminds me of the main reason I called. If you're seriously thinking of moving in with a boyfriend, I wouldn't want to stand in your way, but, otherwise, *please* don't feel you have to move out of the condo."

Susan sighed, her buoyant mood having undergone a swift change. "All those things you said about it in your letter really brought back memories . . . wonderful memories. You're right, the place is not too big to be cozy and yet there's that wonderful openness and fabulous view of the ocean. Don't mind me, Jane—my divorce just went through, and I'm feeling a little down." She went on quickly before Jane could put in a word of sympathy.

"Don't go feeling sorry for me. I'll be fine." Her laugh was a little forced. "As long as there are men like your handsome relative around, little Susan will manage to carry on. But, now, about you. Why go to the bother of finding another place to live if you like where you are? I'd rather have you living in the condo than just have it sit empty—and I couldn't bear the thought of renting it to strangers. If you feel you must pay something, you could pick up the cost of the monthly maintenance and the utilities, if that's not too much." Susan didn't have any inkling of how much it would be or even how much Jane could afford. Such concerns were totally removed from her life. "Does that sound fair to you?"

"Fair," Jane echoed, wanting terribly to accept the offer. "It sounds more than fair. It sounds like an arrangement all in my favor. Are you sure you don't mind, Susan?"

"I wouldn't suggest it if I minded. Besides, I might impose on you sometime and come down for a visit."

"I hope you will."

With this, Susan managed to make Jane feel she was doing Susan a favor by being there, just in case Susan should come. The next day when Jane checked with the management office, she learned that the monthly maintenance fee combined with the electric bill would equal the maximum amount that she would be able to afford for an apartment. Even though she knew that amount of money was negligible to Susan, paying it made Jane feel that she wasn't living on Susan's charity. Undoubtedly Susan had been sensitive enough to know that.

In spite of this further proof of Susan's generosity and also in spite of the glimpse Susan had given into her own sense of failure at having married and divorced twice, Jane didn't feel any better about the thought of James and Susan seeing each other, even though she knew she had no claims on James and no earthly reason to be jealous. He hadn't made any effort to contact her since she had left Islesboro. It was unsupported conjecture on Jane's part that he was waiting very patiently for Jane to fail on her own and come back home to the Patton fold, where he now was uncontested head, since he had taken over support of Lottie.

But there had to be some logical explanation for his putting out all this money for the benefit of an aunt he detested. The cottage had been painted and repaired. The furnace had been rebuilt with new parts. Lottie had a full-time housekeeper living at the cottage.

And now this business about an art critic wanting to see Terry's paintings. Surely James was responsible for that, too, Jane reflected broodingly. What reason could James have for this new altruism if he weren't laying an elaborate trap for Jane? Wasn't he establishing himself as the Patton patriarch with the idea that with beneficence goes control? It all sounded too crazy to say aloud to anyone, but Jane was convinced that James was still in pursuit of her, playing some Machiavellian game.

Well, James was wasting his money if he thought he would get Jane this way. She wasn't going to fail on her own, and she wasn't going to go limping back to

Islesboro, her spirit broken, ready to wed James on his terms. Despite her certainty on this point, Jane still didn't like the thought of James with Susan or, she admitted candidly to herself, with any other woman. She only hoped she intruded into his relationships with the opposite sex as much as he interfered with hers.

That night last summer in James's cottage when Jane had spoken in the aftermath of making love with him, voicing the doubt that any other man would affect her physically the way James did, she hadn't dreamed her words would be quite so prophetic as they were proving to be. Without going out of her way, she had met quite a number of eligible men, some of whom were her neighbors in the condominium complex, others who worked at the large shopping mall. She had gone out on dates with three or four different ones and attended casual parties and weekend barbecues.

But so far not a single one of them could change the rate of her heartbeat with his touch, as James could. She hadn't permitted any caresses more intimate than a good-night kiss because, frankly, she hadn't wanted to. The electricity that had always been there between her and James even when she refused to acknowledge it for what it was, acute sexual awareness, was missing.

But then, it had been missing with Terry, she had to remind herself, yet she had certainly loved Terry and been happy married to him. *You hadn't made love with James, either. You didn't KNOW what it could be like,* came back the unremittingly honest answer.

Faced with the possibility that she might not ever

have a relationship with a man as sexually charged as that she had known with James, Jane nonetheless held out mentally that she had made the right decision in not marrying James. As she had pointed out to James at the time, he didn't love her. They didn't have the necessary substance to their relationship to ensure a good, lasting marriage.

Yes, she had done the right thing, made the best decision, but every time she got a letter from Lottie, with all its news of the improved life James was providing with his money, Jane had the same recurring and bizarre image: James as the Black Knight. Mounted on a white charger and wearing, not metal armor or stately robes, but that abbreviated black swimsuit that had been plastered to his body early last summer when he swam over from the yacht and surprised Jane at her weeding task. Jane had seen him thus in her mind later that same day. The sheer eroticism of the image had excited her then, before she had ever felt him enter her body and possess her totally. It excited her even more now that she had touched James's body with the boldest intimacy, seen its supple beauty naked in the firelight, known the power of arousing him and the ecstasy of total surrender. She had to work harder each time at banishing the image from her mind.

The fantasy certainly wasn't something she could discuss with another person. Even if she had had a friend so intimate that she could mention such personal matters, she would have been reluctant to admit that she blamed James for this dark, sensual figment of her imagination! It was as though he had followed her to Florida with the purpose of undermining her contentment with her new life. Yet there was no way

Jane could make a reprisal, not without establishing some contact with James. And then how could she order him to stop invading her mind in such a provocative guise!

A month after Lottie's letter mentioning the prominent art critic's interest in seeing Terry's paintings, Jane received a manila envelope addressed in Lottie's elegant script. Inside were newspaper clippings, all about the art world's excitement over the discovery of a prodigious talent, Terence Patton, now deceased but leaving behind a precious legacy of artwork. One of the leading art galleries in Boston would hold a showing in late November, eagerly awaited by art lovers.

Along with the clippings was a note from Lottie, who was quite obviously thrilled over the recognition Terry was being given. The older woman's animation came through. Jane read the newspaper clippings through several times and the note as well, oddly disturbed by her reactions. She was pleased for Terry's sake and for Lottie's as well, but her pleasure was mixed with a feeling of having been excluded from what was happening. After all, she was Terry's widow. She had been important in his life and, thus, important in his art.

"You'll be receiving an invitation to the showing in the mail," Lottie wrote. "We hope you'll come."

We. Lottie and James? Who else. They hoped she would come, but if she didn't, everything would proceed very well without her. And just how did they think she could manage to take off to Boston? Surely Lottie and James both should guess that Jane didn't have extra money for airplane tickets and hotel rooms, and she couldn't ask her employer for time off so that she could drive up in the aging Lincoln, which had done well to make the trip down.

Jane wasn't at all happy with the stir of resentment inside her. Somehow she thought she should probably be more philosophical and detached. After all, she was getting what she had wanted, wasn't she? A life of independence in a warmer climate with no obligations to anyone except herself. She should be feeling thankful on Lottie's behalf that life was unfurling some pleasures after a long, bleak stretch. She should be grateful to James that he was making it all possible. She *was* thankful . . . and grateful, but, damn it, she felt left out too. James must have known she would feel excluded. That knowledge only heightened her dissatisfaction.

After she had stewed over the situation a day or two, Jane sat down and wrote Lottie a letter, expressing how glad she was that Terry's art was receiving recognition. As to Jane's attending the showing in Boston, she wouldn't miss it, if at all possible, but there were certain circumstances that made it unlikely that she would be able to get away at that time. Jane was purposefully vague. She was simply laying the groundwork so that Lottie wouldn't be expecting her to appear at the showing.

Once the letter was mailed, Jane felt better and went about her life. The job was working out just as she had hoped it would. The needlework workshops had had good participation and had resulted in increased sales of the kits in the shop. Now Jane was beginning a series of classes for which there would be a modest charge. Her enrollment was heartening as was her employer's growing approval of her efforts.

She had put the art showing out of her mind almost

entirely, when the invitation from the art gallery arrived. A few days later there was a note from Lottie stating that under no circumstances should Jane miss the showing. Lottie would never forgive her if she didn't come up. Enclosed was a check to cover the expense of plane travel. Once Jane arrived in Boston, her hotel reservation would already be made, and she needn't worry about paying it. Lottie would pay for it herself.

Whom did Lottie think she was kidding? James would pay for it, just as he had provided the money to cover this bank draft. Jane held the check gingerly between two fingers, staring down at it, wondering what to do. Lottie would be deeply hurt if Jane didn't come up to Boston. And, truthfully, Jane *wanted* to go. She wanted to be there and hear the praises Terry so well deserved and wouldn't ever hear himself. She wanted to share his triumph with Lottie, who would probably look upon it as the proudest moment of her life.

And why not admit it? *She wanted to see James.* The need had been building up inside her for months to confront him and let him know she was fully aware of what he was up to. Yet it went against her grain to know that James would be financing her trip to Boston.

While Jane was still deliberating as to what to do, she received another missive that helped her to make up her mind. When Susan had telephoned back in September, she hadn't mentioned anything about having shown Jane's sampler to her father, but evidently she had shown it to some high-ranking person in the McGraw Manufacturing Company. The letter that Jane got was from a Randolph McElroy in the design division, inviting her to notify him as to when she could come to Boston and discuss a business offer.

For one wild moment Jane was struck by a suspicion she quickly discounted as being ridiculous. James might be wealthy and influential, but he didn't rule the world. Just because Susan McGraw had mentioned meeting James, it didn't mean that James was wielding power with the McGraw Manufacturing Company just to make sure Jane came up to Boston for the gallery showing. Susan had been very firm on the point that not even she could pressure her hard-headed businessman of a father into any deal that wasn't advantageous for the company. No, Mr. McGraw or someone else in a decision-making capacity, probably this Randolph McElroy, must have been impressed by the sampler Susan had bought at the crafts co-op in Islesboro and thought that the design might have market potential.

Now there was no question about it. Jane had to go to Boston. The Terence Patton exhibit opening, by invitation only, was on Friday evening. She would try to get her appointment for earlier in the day. Then on Saturday evening there was a formal dinner hosted by a noted art patron. On Sunday Jane would return to Lauderdale and be ready to return to work on Monday morning.

Instead of writing, Jane telephoned Lottie. It was strange that once Jane had decided to go to Boston and knew that she would see Lottie again in just weeks, she was eager to hear the sound of her mother-in-law's voice, eager to talk about the excitement ahead. Lottie rattled on, sounding incredibly like her old self in that long-ago time when gala social events had been everyday occurrences. Jane felt her own enthusiasm rise.

She kept waiting for James's name to come up so she could verify that he would be at the opening, but, quite astonishingly, Lottie made no mention whatever of James. Finally Jane couldn't stand it any longer and asked offhandedly, "I suppose James will be there."

"I know for certain that he was invited," Lottie answered unhesitatingly, with just a trace of her old disapproval, which, under the circumstances, Jane found incredible. Curiosity got the best of discretion.

"Don't you see James? Talk to him?"

"Why, no. How did you get that impression? I haven't seen James since you left Islesboro last summer. But I'm assuming he will be at the reception, since you will be there." The last statement, quite blatantly coy, came as a relief to Jane. She had begun to wonder if she wasn't mistaken in believing Lottie and James were in league against her. But why would Lottie lie about not having seen James? Of course, she hadn't said she hadn't *talked* to James or corresponded with him.

No, there was definitely a conspiracy between those two. The fact that Lottie's attitude toward James hadn't noticeably changed, in spite of his generosity toward her, was good indication that James's feelings toward his aunt hadn't changed either. He wasn't making her life easier out of affection or simple human kindness. James had to have an ulterior motive, and it must have something to do with Jane. In spite of the fact that he had sworn he would never ask

Jane to marry him again, wasn't he still harboring that old obsession to make her his wife?

Jane thought that he was, but after the telephone conversation with Lottie there was the tiniest uncertainty that she might be wrong in her interpretation of James's actions. As the date for her trip to Boston grew nearer, she grew impatient and restless. She told herself she was simply nervous about the appointment with the McGraw company executive, but she knew all along it was more than that.

Before she could put down roots here in Florida and make a life for herself that would allow for lasting relationships, she had to have this thing out with James once and for all. She couldn't have him haunting her thoughts, going along on her dates with other men like a watchful, patient shadow, there to see that nothing happened.

But what if she got to Boston and discovered that all of this psychological entrapment was in her own mind? What if James had meant every word of his ultimatum to her last summer and hadn't given her a thought since?

What then?

When James checked with his personal answering service for messages, he was annoyed to learn of the call from Lottie, guessing at once what it was about. The exhibit opening in Boston. He hadn't made the requested reply to indicate whether he would attend the champagne reception on Friday evening or heeded the RSVP clause on the invitation to the private dinner the following evening.

It was definitely a violation of etiquette that he

hadn't attended to either of those matters. James knew he hadn't forgotten. That awareness annoyed him as much as his aunt's telephone call.

He sat for long minutes in the study of his Manhattan apartment, gazing down at Central Park. The branches of the deciduous trees were almost completely bare, with just a few dry rusty leaves hanging on. Why did he live here, in the midst of this huge impersonal city, when he could live anywhere in the world?

Why live anywhere else?

James reached for the telephone and punched out the digits of his aunt's telephone number, knowing as he did so that he was violating his pact with himself. Giving her money and taking over her financial affairs was one thing; subjecting himself to her personality and presence was another.

"James, I'm sorry to bother you," Lottie apologized at once after James had briefly identified himself. "I know you're a very busy man."

"Not that busy," James put in, wanting her to get to the point. He preferred the old open antagonism to this phony ingratiating manner. Whatever he had done for her, he had done because he could and had to, if he wanted to live with himself, not for any gratitude and certainly not to encourage friendly relations.

"I talked to Mr. Evanson at the art gallery today. He was telling me that nearly everyone who was invited to the reception has accepted." Lottie dropped a little pause. "I do hope you'll be there, James. It would mean so much to me. And to Jane, I'm sure. After all, you're a member of the family.

When Jane called a couple of weeks ago to say that she would be able to come, she asked if you would be there." Another discreet pause.

It was on the tip of James's tongue to make a sarcastic comment to the effect that Jane was probably hoping to determine that he *wouldn't* be there, but he managed to restrain himself and then Lottie was talking on.

"At first, Jane wasn't coming. She made all sorts of vague excuses, but I knew the real reason. The poor girl couldn't afford the price of a plane ticket. So I sent her the money and promised to pay for her hotel room. She called as soon as she received my check in the mail. James, I could read between the words. She's terribly homesick. It's just pride that keeps her from admitting she made a mistake. I don't expect her to go back to Florida once she gets back up here, where she belongs."

James found Lottie's pitying tone of voice so offensive on Jane's behalf that he dropped his guard. "That's not the news I've heard. According to Jane's friend, Susan McGraw, Jane has a job she really likes and more invitations to parties than she can keep up with." As soon as the words were out, James wished it were physically possible to kick himself in the rear. Lottie's preening satisfaction at his sharp tone came oozing over the telephone line.

"I'll just have to see for myself." Lottie was careful not to sound argumentative. "One look at Jane, and I'll know whether she's happy. It seems like such a long time she's been gone. . . ."

God knows she didn't have to tell James it had been a long time. The thought of seeing Jane was an ache inside him. His aunt had called and wakened it on purpose. Well, he wouldn't give her the instant satisfaction of knowing she had succeeded all the way.

"I'll just have to see how my schedule works out at the last minute," he told her coolly.

After he had broken the connection he didn't hang up the receiver. He called the art gallery in Boston and confirmed that he would be attending the exhibit opening, with a guest. Before he could make his next call he had to look up the phone number, since it wasn't one he called often enough recently to have committed to memory.

"Belinda, James Patton here. You're right, it has been a long time. Last June, to be exact. Of course I remember. No, I haven't been spying on any neighbors with binoculars lately. Come on, I really did have some important business come up so that I had to jump ship and let the rest of you finish out the cruise without me. Honest. Say, enough about that. I plan to be in town next weekend."

Belinda pouted a bit before she agreed to accompany James to the exhibit of his cousin's paintings, but there wasn't ever any real chance of her refusing him, even though he had neglected her for half a year. In Belinda's book, James was one of the sexiest men she knew. And she hadn't exactly been languishing in his absence either.

James had to restrain his impatience to get off the phone. He supposed he should feel some compunction for asking a woman out when he didn't have a shred of interest in her company, but then, he found it difficult to muster interest in the company of any woman these days, no matter how attractive or personable she might be.

The truth was that he was still hung up on Jane, but he didn't want to go to that damned reception with his tongue hanging out, like a stray dog hoping for favors. It might be cowardly of him to want some protection, but that's precisely what Belinda would be. With another woman on his arm he would be safe—not so much from Jane but from *himself* and what he might say or do.

Chapter Ten

*I*t was cold and gray in Boston when Jane arrived on Friday morning. So far there hadn't been a big winter snowstorm to leave its mantle of white. The buildings and trees all looked naked and exposed to Jane's eyes as she gazed out the taxi window on the ride from the airport to her hotel.

She thought of past times, when she had been here in Boston during the first major snowstorm, and her blood tingled with remembered exhilaration. Inevitably there was inconvenience, interference with the regular comings and goings of people's lives, unfortunate and even tragic mishaps, but it was exciting and awesome too.

Jane smiled, recapturing the sting of snowflakes flung against her cheeks, borne along currents of raw wind. The sensation brought immediately to mind the Christmas season. People rushing along the streets and hurrying into stores where there was light and warmth and music. Of course, in those days when she would be here in Boston for Christmas, she would be bundled warmly in a fur coat, a matching furry hat on her head, and fur-lined boots on her feet. Wealth tended to insulate one from the weather as well as from many of life's other unpleasantnesses.

The weather forecast promised the skies wouldn't dump that first big load of snow on Boston this particular weekend. The practical part of Jane was relieved at that assurance. Certainly she didn't want the airport to be closed down and travel in and out of the city paralyzed, as could easily happen with a major storm.

But another part of her was sorry. *I think I'm homesick!* she realized with a shock, and then saw at once that it was true. She missed New England. Or at least she missed its seasons. When September had arrived in Florida, something inside her had longed for vivid fall colors, in particular the flaming reds and golds of the maples and birches. There had been that sense of expectation for signs of winter that weren't going to happen in the land of sunshine. She wasn't going to awaken one morning to discover the first frost. There was no fireplace in the Lauderdale condominium, no racks of neatly stacked firewood outside. By late September Jane finally realized the reason for her growing feeling that the lovely, comfortable rooms in the condo lacked a core. Everything was designed for a movement outward, the whole year round, whereas Jane's internal clock had alerted her that it was time for seeking shelter and warmth inside.

Now, as she exchanged a few remarks with the taxi driver, whose Irish brogue fell pleasantly on her ears,

Jane acknowledged that she was experiencing a sense of homecoming that was understandable under the circumstances. She had been born right here in Boston and lived most of her life in New England. This attack of nostalgia was in no way an admission that she had made a mistake in going south, she told herself firmly. For she definitely hadn't made a mistake. In two days she would be flying back to Lauderdale and no doubt would be more than ready to step out into seventy-degree sunshine.

"I would have to *live* in Boston!" she heard herself exclaiming aloud a mere two hours later as she sat across from Randolph McElroy in his staid, wood-paneled office. Neatly arranged on the surface of his polished mahogany desk was the embroidered sampler Susan had bought from Jane last summer, along with several other original pieces Jane had brought up to Boston with her.

Neither Randolph McElroy nor his office environs were what Jane had expected. He looked more like a barrister than someone in charge of creative design. Strengthening that impression were the excellent Hogarth prints adorning the walls of his office. *No wonder the needlework kits the McGraw Manufacturing Company produced were so boring!* Earlier in the interview Jane had been bold enough to suggest that there were few kits on the market these days to challenge the skilled needleworker.

"You wouldn't necessarily have to reside in Boston, but certainly in the area," McElroy replied reasonably. "It would be necessary for you to work closely with other people in our kit-design department as well as with technicians in production. As I've already said, your designs are excellent, but they would need to be simplified. There are also considerations as to cost of producing a kit. That bears directly upon the price of the kit, of course. And then you would need to be involved with the market research. We don't go blindly into producing a new kit design without testing its potential appeal to our customers. As I'm sure you'll agree, it would be necessary for you to live within an easily accessible distance, Mrs. Patton."

"I see," Jane murmured, overwhelmed. She hadn't come to this appointment expecting an interview for a position at all, and certainly not for a position as complex as this one sounded. "Actually, Mr. McElroy, I was under the impression that you might just want to buy some of my designs outright. What kind of salary are we talking about?" So far he hadn't mentioned money.

Randolph McElroy was well prepared for the question. He opened a legal-size folder and took several pages from it that he handed across to Jane. It was a contract stating her basic starting salary with the company and outlining her share of profits earned on her original designs. Written in legalese, Jane found the document hopelessly bewildering even after McElroy had gone through all the figures with her.

"I don't know. I'll have to think about it," she said uncertainly. Upon her arrival in Boston she had been feeling nostalgic about New England and snow, but did she really want to move back? Was the offer really a good one? The salary was much more than she was currently earning, but it didn't sound like enough for a job as demanding as McElroy had made this one sound. Would her share of profits make up the difference? Was her option cut and dried, either to take or turn down the offer? Or was it expected that she would negotiate for better terms? Jane simply had no way of knowing the answers to any of these questions.

"I'll give the offer some thought and let you know," she promised, trying to sound interested but noncommittal and not as agitated as she felt. "Is there any time limit I should keep in mind?"

McElroy made a neat steeple with his hands and considered. "We would like to know your decision within a reasonable time. Shall we say one month?"

Back at her hotel Jane ate a late lunch in the coffee shop and pondered the entire meeting, no, *interview* it had turned out to be. She was unequipped to trust her own judgment about people and situations in the business world, but Randolph McElroy certainly had not seemed to *care* one way or the other whether she accepted or refused the offer he made her. Was Susan responsible for Jane's being made the offer after all?

At least she had some time to think about it. Nick Olson, who lived in the condominium next to hers, was an attorney. She'd get him to look the contract over and give his opinion of it. What she really needed, though, was the advice of someone who knew business, preferably even somebody with contacts in Eastern manufacturing who could tell her if the offer was a fair one or if she would be selling herself short.

Somebody like James.

But could she trust James to tell her the truth? Wouldn't he give her the advice that would bring her back north, within his sphere of power?

After she had finished her lunch, Jane spent the rest of the afternoon browsing through shops and department stores. In the back of her mind she was looking for something new and stunning to wear to the reception that evening, but she knew she couldn't afford to buy a new outfit. The ankle-length velvet skirt and silk blouse she had brought along would have to do. They were old but timeless because of their classic styling and excellent quality. At least she had a new hairdo, a 'boy' cut that had felt really strange at first, since she had been accustomed for years to pinning her hair up into the topknot from which it invariably straggled free.

It was six o'clock by the time she returned to her hotel to find that Lottie had checked in during Jane's absence and had left a message. Her room was on the floor below Jane's, but they would not be going to the gallery together that evening since Lottie was invited out for cocktails and an early supper and would go from her hostess's home to the gallery. Since James knew that both Lottie and Jane would be staying at this hotel, Lottie thought he might call and offer to escort Jane to the showing.

Jane hadn't a doubt that Lottie had probably made that suggestion to James, but he didn't call. She took a taxi alone to the gallery, glad that she was to go a little early. Jane and Lottie, widow and mother of the artist, were to be there when the other guests arrived.

It was a shock at first to see Terry's paintings on display. They were more powerful and more disturbing in the chambers of the gallery than they had been in his studio at the cottage in Islesboro. Here they were lighted and arranged by experts so that each large canvas made its bold impact.

Jane felt instantly protective on Terry's behalf and hoped that no one said anything critical in her hearing because she didn't know how she would react. It was simply impossible for her to be objective about what had been an extension of Terry himself. He had put his life and soul into these paintings. It seemed a violation of privacy to expose them to the view of total strangers who might be unsympathetic.

Fortunately Jane didn't have time to dwell on her first reaction to the exhibit. Lottie was there, regal in her long gown, beaming in the midst of a small group of select gallery patrons who had come early. These included the earlier supper party. At the first sight of Jane, Lottie swept her into the group and made introductions.

From that point on Jane had no time for introspection. She was too busy replying to introductions and listening to all the superlatives about Terry's work. More people began to arrive, and it seemed that everyone wanted to meet the widow of the artistic genius who had hidden himself away in the Maine woods. Some of the conversation that buzzed around her was too technical or erudite to mean much to her, but she thrilled to words such as "powerful," "sensitive," "original."

By the time the first hour had slipped past, she was fully reassured that the overwhelming reaction to Terry's paintings was admiration, much of it verging on awe. Jane was able to relax her guard. It was then that she started looking for James and wondering if he was coming at all. Perhaps he had even come and left without her knowledge, altogether a possibility given the labyrinthine arrangement of the gallery's chambers.

Jane could imagine James arriving and finding the situation too distasteful to endure—it wasn't likely he would take any pleasure in the adulation being heaped upon his dead cousin—but she did find it difficult to believe that James could come here and leave without making his presence known to her. When she finally did see him, he was across the room from her but not obviously headed in her direction. Probably he hadn't even noticed she was there because all his attention was focused upon the companion draped across his arm, a tall blonde stunningly dressed in black. Jane was so taken aback that for a long moment she openly stared. It hadn't once occurred to her that James would show up with a date.

"Er, yes," she said to the stout matron she had just been introduced to. "My husband spent three years studying in France before he came back and lived permanently in Maine. . . ." *Just what was James up to?*

Jane was undecided as to what she should do. Should she pretend she hadn't seen him and wait until they drifted close to each other to speak? Should she approach him directly and get the inevitable meeting over with? For a minute or two she tried the former but found her powers of concentration so scattered that she couldn't hold the questions and comments of her companions in her head long enough to make sensible replies. Everyone was having to say things twice. Suddenly she knew she couldn't stand the suspense of waiting.

"Excuse me," she murmured, and made her way across the room. Halfway there, she knew James had been aware of her the whole time and had been keeping track of her movements. He looked around before he had any cause to be alerted to her approach. There wasn't the mildest surprise in his dark eyes, nor much else that she could read other than guardedness.

"Hello, James. I'm glad you could come," she said formally when she had reached them. Her eyes shifted to the blond woman while she waited politely to be introduced.

"Belinda Mason, this is my cousin by marriage, Jane Patton." James matched her formality. "How are you, Jane? It looks as if the exhibit is a great success. That must be very gratifying to both you and my aunt." James watched the color come up in her cheeks beneath the light tan. She looked marvelous. He liked the new cropped hairdo. It made her hazel eyes seem even larger, her fine bone structure more pronounced, the shape of her mouth more voluptuous. He was intensely aware of every slight movement of her lips as they tightened briefly and then formed her next stiff words.

"We are very proud, of course."

Belinda Mason was not the stereotypical beautiful but dumb blonde. She'd known something was up as soon as they'd arrived at the gallery tonight. Underneath the debonair manner James was tense and distracted. Now her woman's instinct told her that the "something up" had to do with Jane. James's arm had tightened into steel under her hand a minute ago and then Jane had materialized next to them with her stilted greeting.

Suddenly Belinda made some connections that had not clicked into place before now. The deceased cousin whose paintings were on display had lived the last years of his life a recluse on his mother's summer estate in Maine, on Penobscot Bay. Earlier Belinda had asked idly where James's summer cottage was in relationship to his aunt's and been told that the two properties were adjacent. With Jane's appearance

Belinda suddenly knew without question whom James had been spying upon with the binoculars last summer from the cockpit of the yacht when they had been anchored offshore from his Islesboro cottage. She also thought she knew the nature of that urgent "business" that had come up unexpectedly, forcing James to cut short his presence aboard the yacht when he had been the one to organize the cruise in the first place.

Belinda had been "used" tonight. The realization wasn't the most pleasant, but then, she had been used before and, similarly, done her own share of male exploitation when it suited her purposes. In this particular instance she couldn't determine exactly what her role was, whether she was to be the "other woman" to raise jealousy or whether she was to serve as a shield and "protect" James. Oddly enough, she half-suspected the latter. If her intuition was correct, this was the first hint of vulnerability she had ever glimpsed in James, whose self-containment had always seemed impregnable.

"I do admire your husband's art," Belinda told Jane, turning upon her a smiling glance that held more than a little curiosity. Privately she found the paintings rather too overwhelming. They were the sort of thing one could appreciate in a gallery but not imagine hanging over one's living room sofa. Certainly it was difficult to imagine the man who had painted them as the husband of this attractive but quite ordinary young woman. "Now, if you two will excuse me, I see someone I really *must* say hello to." With a gentle squeeze of James's arm Belinda glided away, quite deliberately leaving him in the lurch.

Her leavetaking took them both so by surprise that neither could think of anything to say for a second or two. James, not surprisingly, was the first to recover his aplomb. Now that Belinda had turned traitor, he called up the presence of his dead cousin to take her place.

"What do you think?" He glanced around the room whose expensive lighting and subdued decor were an artwork in themselves. Well-dressed art patrons with champagne glasses in their hands greeted one another familiarly and carried on animated conversations in clusters before each of Terry's paintings. After the newspaper coverage of the last two months, and after tonight, anyone who purported to know anything about contemporary American oil painting would be familiar with the name Terence Patton.

Jane followed his glance. "I find this all hard to believe. One moment Terry is completely unknown, and then all of a sudden he's like some kind of art celebrity." Jane shook her head. Recalling her initial feelings upon arrival at the gallery that evening, she smiled ruefully. "I nearly panicked when I first got here and saw Terry's paintings so prominently displayed that they seemed to jump right off the walls. Before—well, you saw them in his studio. They looked as if they 'belonged' there. Honestly, James, I felt like a mother, afraid nobody would play with her child his first day at school! I knew how much Terry had put of himself into these paintings. I was so afraid the people would come and wouldn't like his work." Jane made the admission in a shamed tone, hesitated, and then confessed something she'd never put into words before. "I've never known whether Terry was 'good' or not. It didn't really seem to matter since he painted just for himself anyway."

Now that James had raised the specter of his cousin

and created the old threesome, he had to cope with the familiar dark emotions that rose inside his breast: jealousy, resentment, anger. He was the survivor, the one standing here with Jane tonight, and yet Terry was still the cousin in favor.

"I'm not much of an art connoisseur myself, but I knew he was good the minute I saw these." James jerked his head sideways toward the painting in front of which they stood and then noticed that quite a crowd had drifted up around them. Taking Jane's arm, he threaded his way through the people to a less crowded spot farther along.

Jane was working up her nerve for the real question she was about to ask. Eventually she would get around to verifying that James was behind Terry's discovery by the art world and ask him why he'd made his cousin's recognition possible, but first there was something she wanted to know more.

"James, do you . . . like Terry's paintings?"

James had been expecting the other *obvious* questions, not this. It was only Jane's sharp intake of breath that made him realize his fingers had tightened on her arm like a vise.

"Do I *like* these?" he repeated incredulously, dropping his hand from her arm and glancing at the nearest painting before returning his gaze to her face. "How in God's name can anybody *like* or *not like* these paintings? It's like asking if I like feeling every powerful emotion a human being can feel, all at the same time. Anger, joy, hatred, ecstasy . . . love."

Without knowing what he intended, James took her arm again and started them moving through the room. Jane went along unresistingly. James's words had affected her deeply. More than any of the knowledgeable comments she had heard tonight, he had in layman's language summed up the impact of Terry's paintings.

The door at the far end of the room was painted the same muted color as the walls. It could have passed notice completely except for the discreet prohibition: AUTHORIZED PERSONNEL ONLY, which James ignored. Beyond the door was a corridor. Once they were in the corridor, James paused a second, sucking in a deep breath, and then ushered Jane immediately through an open door into a small room that was evidently a lounge for gallery personnel. It was furnished with several sofas and armchairs and had kitchen equipment along one wall, including a refrigerator, coffeemaker, and microwave oven.

"James, are you all right?" Jane inquired anxiously, seeing the unhealthy pallor of his face.

James dropped her arm and took several steps away from her, drawing in another deep breath. The enormous relief of stepping into these mundane surroundings was similar to the way he'd felt last summer emerging from his aunt's cottage into the fresh air after seeing his cousin's paintings for the first time. And Jane had wanted to know if he *liked* them!

"I'm fine," he said tersely, turning around to face her, his guard raised again. "I just don't like crowds, that's all."

Jane had to cope with a wave of disappointment. She had wanted to tell him how his comments about Terry's paintings had penetrated right to the quick of her own feelings about them, but she couldn't now, not with James regarding her with that closed, watchful expression.

"Why did you do it, James?" she asked quietly. "If

it makes you physically ill to be in the same room with Terry's paintings, why did you send that art critic out to Aunt Lottie's cottage? Why did you set all this in motion?" She gestured behind her, back toward the door through which they'd just come.

James looked past her at the door, his eyes narrowed, as though he were seeing through it and visualizing the room beyond. "It was only a matter of time anyway," he said matter-of-factly, indirectly confirming her assumption that he *was* responsible for Terry's discovery. "Unless something happened to destroy the paintings, they would have ended up in the public eye sooner or later. I knew that the moment you took me into his studio that day last summer."

"Is that the reason then? You knew the paintings were good, and you didn't want to take the chance they might be destroyed?" Jane didn't mean to sound so frankly skeptical.

James's gaze transferred quickly to her. "Why is it so important for you to know my motive, Jane?" he asked shrewdly. "Isn't it enough for you that all those people out there are admiring Terry's work, hailing him as a genius?"

"Why, I think it's natural for me to wonder. . . ." Jane returned defensively, uncomfortable under the spotlight of those dark, searching eyes. "After all, there was never any love lost between you and Terry. You're hardly the one I'd expect to bring recognition to him."

"Maybe I'm doing whatever I can to make up for past unkindness," James suggested, carefully noncommittal but not mocking. "Maybe I just consider it my duty as a human being to bring to the notice of the world a great talent. Maybe I don't even know my reason myself, Jane. But in case you're thinking there was some ulterior motive, I can assure you that I don't stand to gain anything personally from that exhibit out there. Very few people know I had anything to do with it. And whatever proceeds come from sale of the paintings will go to you and my aunt."

"James, I didn't think you had done it for *money!*" Jane protested.

"Just what *did* you think was my motive, Jane?" he asked softly and noted the color suffusing her face. In spite of himself, James felt his heart start to pound as he took a step toward her and then another, seeing the answer to his question in her eyes. "Did you think I did it for you? Perhaps hoping to make you grateful, convince you that my character had changed for the better?" Now there was light mockery in his voice, but it couldn't cover the caressing tone that told Jane he was reacting just as she was to their nearness. As he brought his hands up and lightly grasped her shoulders, moving them ever so slightly over her silk blouse, Jane faced the truth that she had come to Boston for more than answers. She had come to have him touch her again, take her into his arms . . . make love to her.

"Did you, James . . . do it for me?" she asked, tilting back her head and slowly bringing her hands up to rest her fingertips against the pleated front of his white shirt.

"No, Jane." He shook his head abruptly to emphasize the denial to himself as well to her. "You had nothing whatever to do with it." The whole discussion was fast seeming irrelevant. The warmth of her flesh underneath the silk was burning his palms, and the heat was spreading through him. The need to kiss those softly parted lips within such easy reach was a savage ache inside. Why resist? What harm would it do to take her into his arms? James knew his reasoning was no better than an alcoholic's deceiving himself into believing he could "take just one drink," but his head was starting to lower and Jane's eyes were fluttering closed when a movement behind her caught his attention.

The door across the corridor opened, and Belinda stepped through. He had brought her to the exhibit to protect him from exactly what was happening and promptly forgotten her very existence when she moved out of his sight. Now, as he dropped his hands away from Jane's shoulders, he knew Belinda had proved his salvation, but he felt cheated rather than grateful.

Belinda took the scene in with a glance. "Here you are," she announced, moving to the open door of the lounge. "I've had enough modern culture for one night, James, darling. If you're not ready to leave yet, I'll just take a taxi."

The sound of Belinda's voice took Jane completely unawares, since her back was to the door. She drew herself quickly erect and tried to compose her face as she turned around, but Belinda's knowing blue eyes took in Jane's expression, which was that of a woman who had been about to be kissed.

"I'm quite ready to leave," James assured Belinda quickly. He was fast recovering and realizing what a close call it had been. "Jane and I just escaped the crush a few minutes to talk over old times."

Belinda shrugged as if to say he should suit himself

and was about to turn away when James stopped her.
"Wait. We're coming too." He looked at Jane inquiringly. "Ready to rejoin the throngs?"

Jane's recovery hadn't been as quick. She was in no
condition to go back into the gallery showrooms and
mingle with all those people. Nor could she believe
that James actually intended to leave immediately
with Belinda. There was too much between James and
herself that still had to be settled. After what had
been about to happen just now, how could he walk
away and leave her standing here?

"I'll just stay here a minute longer," she said,
meeting his eyes accusingly.

James inclined his head in acceptance of her wish to
remain. "As you wish. It was good seeing you again,
Jane." With those polite words of leavetaking he
headed for the door.

Jane started after him incredulously. Surely he
didn't intend not to see her again while she was here
in Boston!

"*James—*"

He stopped short just as he reached Belinda, who
was taking it all in with bored interest. She knew from
the way James grabbed her arm that he wasn't as cool
as he looked.

Jane hadn't meant to blurt his name out in that
reproachful tone. She had simply responded to the
urgent realization that once he left the gallery tonight,
she wouldn't know how to get in touch with him.

"I just wondered if you'd be at the dinner tomorrow
night," she said with as much dignity as she could
muster.

"*Ouch,*" Belinda muttered, and slipped her hand
protestingly over James's grip on her arm. She'd have

black-and-blue marks there tomorrow. "He's going to the dinner," she told Jane with blithe irony. "He wouldn't miss it for anything. Right, James?"

James frowned at Belinda, loosening his hold on her arm. Now he was regretting his decision to leave with her. He wanted more than anything in the world to stay behind with Jane.

Jane's pride had finally come to her rescue. She didn't like the image of herself grasping at the coat-tails of a man who was trying to leave with another woman.

"I was just curious, that's all. If you won't be there, then I'll tell you good-bye now. My flight back to Fort Lauderdale is early Sunday morning."

"I'll be at the dinner. It had slipped my mind," James lied. He hadn't accepted the invitation, but Belinda was right. He wouldn't be able to bypass the opportunity to see Jane again, although it was against his better judgment.

"I'll see you there then." Jane made a polite dismissive gesture. "Please, don't let me detain you any longer."

As soon as the two of them had gone, Jane's proud composure deserted her. She backed up and sank down on a vinyl-upholstered sofa. The meeting with James tonight hadn't gone at all according to her expectations. All these months had she been wrong about him . . . terribly wrong? Was it true that his motive for bringing Terry's paintings to the attention of the art world had nothing to do with Jane, as he claimed? Could his generosity toward Lottie not be calculated to get Jane into his clutches as she'd thought?

These possibilities were deeply unsettling. Jane told

herself that she was simply disturbed that her perception of things might have been so far off the mark. And, after all, she wasn't yet *sure* she'd been wrong. Tomorrow night she would have a chance to talk to James again, ask him questions, read his reactions as well as hear his answers. Until then she would reserve judgment.

When Jane and Lottie returned to the hotel late that evening, Lottie was exhausted but still wound up.

"You must come to my room awhile," she insisted to Jane. "We haven't had a chance to talk."

Jane knew even as she acquiesced that Lottie's sole topic of conversation would be the exhibit and Terry's triumph that evening. The older woman rattled on, not noticing at first the forced quality of Jane's responses, but finally she fixed a reproachful gaze upon Jane's face.

"Aren't you happy for Terence's sake? After all, he was your husband—"

"Of course, I'm happy for Terry," Jane demurred. "I'm just tired, Aunt Lottie, that's all." Jane knew it would be pointless to make any recriminations of her own. She hadn't seen her mother-in-law since last June. There was a great deal they could be talking about besides the exhibit. Lottie hadn't asked a single question about Jane's job or indicated any interest in Jane's life in Florida. If she had, Jane would have told her about the interview that morning and the job offer from the McGraw Company.

"I *wonder . . .*" Lottie said musingly as a speculative expression crossed her face. "That was a stunning woman James was escorting tonight. Just remember, Jane, I warned you that he wouldn't be patient forever."

Jane's first instinct was to pretend indifference and change the subject, but then it occurred to her that here was an opportunity to get at the truth from a different direction. Why was Lottie so certain James was waiting patiently in the background?

"Aunt Lottie, last June when I was packing to leave Islesboro, you telephoned James. Could you tell me *exactly* what the two of you said to each other?"

Lottie looked pleased, putting an obvious interpretation upon Jane's interest: Jane must finally be coming to her senses. "I don't remember *exactly* what I said to James or he said to me. I told him you were packing to leave and asked him to help me stop you from acting so foolishly. He told me to let you go. He said I should give you the car and whatever money I had in the bank."

Jane waited, sure that there had to be more, but Lottie held her gaze steadily, her eyebrows slightly elevated. "Is that *all?*" Jane pressed skeptically.

"That's all that was actually said."

Jane stared hard at the older woman, but there wasn't a trace of evasiveness. Lottie was obviously telling the truth. Jane shook her head in puzzlement.

"Aunt Lottie, if that's all James said, why is it that you think—" Jane broke off at the delicate distaste on her mother-in-law's face.

"Jane—*really*. Do you have to have everything drawn in black and white? James has been most generous. As you well know, the Patton family was never close, at least not in my time. Of course James is interested in you. He always was. You must have been aware of that." Lottie was mildly reproving.

Jane opened her mouth to protest that there had to be *more* than just this supposition on Lottie's part, but then she closed it again, facing the truth. It was a mere assumption on Lottie's part that James's "interest" in Jane was the explanation for his generosity.

The older woman was watching her with a sharpening gaze. "Jane, didn't James ask you to marry him last summer? It was my understanding that he intended to do so."

Jane met the concern in the older woman's eyes and glanced away. "He didn't exactly 'ask' me, Aunt Lottie. He 'assumed' I would be glad to marry him, but I told him I had no intention of marrying anyone then." James's faulty assurance that Jane would marry him had been primarily Lottie's doing, but there didn't seem much reason to plow up that old ground.

"So *there*," Lottie declared a little impatiently, as if she couldn't figure out what Jane was worrying about.

"Aunt Lottie, when I turned James down, he told me I should wait and think my answer over. He said it would be the last time he would ever ask me." Jane had been watching Lottie closely. The dismay on the older woman's face was genuine. Lottie hadn't known of James's ultimatum.

"Men *say* things out of pride. . . ." Lottie didn't sound at all convinced. Jane squared her shoulders under the glint of pity in the older woman's blue eyes.

"It really doesn't matter," Jane stated briskly, standing up in preparation for leaving. "I wasn't ready to marry James—or anyone else, for that matter—last summer. It was the right decision for me to make." She took a step toward the door. "I'm very happy in Florida, Aunt Lottie. My job has worked out very well. I'll have to tell you about it tomorrow. And I have other exciting news too. A big business opportunity. But I'm tired now, and I know you're tired too. It's been a wonderful night for both of us, hasn't it?"

"Yes, it has, dear," Lottie said gently, getting up and coming over to Jane. "A wonderful night for our Terry." The emotion in her face and voice brought tears to Jane's throat. As Lottie hugged her close, Jane had her first real feeling of having come home, but she dreaded the question she thought Lottie would be asking her: When was Jane coming home to Islesboro?

"Aunt Lottie, I've missed you," she whispered, overcome with sadness.

"I've missed you, too, child." Lottie patted her back tenderly. "I know I've been very selfish where you've been concerned, Jane. That's the reason I have to say something I pray you won't misunderstand. You will always have a home with me at any time that you choose, but I won't ask you to come back to Islesboro unless it's what you really want, dear. You must do what is best for *you.*"

"Thank you—" Jane pulled away, knowing that she was very close to breaking down and causing an emotional scene that neither of them wanted. "Good night, now. I'll see you tomorrow, and we can talk."

In her own room Jane did break down. It was a reaction to the whole evening, not just the scene between Lottie and herself just now. The pool of sadness inside her seemed to spring from an inexhaustible source as she wept for all of them—Terry, James, Lottie, herself . . . even Old Mr. Patton, whom she'd barely known. They'd all been bound together by the Patton name and tangled relationships that brought all too little joy. Now Terry and his grandfather were dead. Lottie would live out the rest of her life alone with her memories. James would continue to live a life built around a bitter core that was the past he couldn't put behind him.

And Jane . . . What would happen to her? Tonight her future was a blur she saw through the sheet of her tears. The only dominant impression was that she faced it alone.

Chapter Eleven

*T*he next morning when Jane awoke and recalled the emotional storm of the night before, she concluded that it had been a needed release. First, there had been the attack of nostalgia at returning to Boston, then the surprise of Randolph McElroy's offer, which demanded her to make important decisions she didn't feel prepared to make, later in the evening the shock of seeing Terry's paintings displayed for the eyes of the world, followed by the disturbing meeting with James, and then, the finale of the long day, what amounted to a reconciliation with Lottie. Good heavens, hadn't there been enough strain, all in one day, to cause her to break down? How much could one mere human be expected to take?

As she dressed for the day ahead, Jane didn't look upon life in general or her own future with the dark despair that had overwhelmed her the night before.

Already she was greatly adjusted to the idea that both she and Lottie had quite possibly been living for six months with some faulty assumptions about James that, once removed, made him a much better person than they'd given him credit for being. If he hadn't been charitable toward his aunt and his dead cousin with the ulterior motive of establishing claim to Jane, then he must have more admirable motives, mustn't he?

Maybe James wasn't her "black knight" after all. . . .

This reflection was like the click of a switch immediately throwing upon the screen of her mind the now familiar image she'd first seen last June: James sitting up on a fancy war charger of medieval adventure tales but wearing only the brief black swimsuit. The fantasy never lost its element of bizarre eroticism nor did it ever fail to heighten her sense of being a woman. But today Jane wasn't sure about the expression in the dark eyes of the man whose image she held in her mind. "Don't fight me, Jane, I've come to get you," it had always seemed to say. The sexual promise was as strong as the threat of physical intimidation.

Jane banished the image and replaced it with one that was real: James as she had seen him last night, impeccably correct in his dark evening attire with a stunning woman at his side. There had been no burning invitation in his eyes as he looked up and spotted Jane heading across the room in his direction. He'd been guarded and aloof, and at the first opportunity to leave the gallery, he had bolted. His behavior was anything but that of a determined suitor.

And yet the sexual attraction had been there, strong as ever. James had been about to kiss her when

Belinda interrupted. Jane remembered the feel of his hands on her shoulders, the intoxicating closeness of their bodies, the sharpening anticipation as his head had slowly bent toward hers . . . the sense of having been cheated when he halted abruptly and then stepped away.

Flinging her hairbrush down with a little muttered profanity, Jane wondered if he would bring Belinda or some other woman to the dinner tonight. She hoped he wouldn't. It would be her only opportunity to talk to him again before she returned to Florida. Perhaps they could even go somewhere afterward.

James didn't bring a date to the formal dinner that night, which was held in a banquet room of one of the finest old Boston hotels, but he might as well have for all the chance Jane got to talk privately with him. The guests were all art patrons, and once again the talk centered around art in general and Terry's paintings in particular. At dinner she was seated several chairs down from James and on the same side of the long table so that she couldn't even exchange glances with him.

It was a frustrating situation for her. She was thrilled for Terry's sake that he was getting all this recognition, but that didn't mean she was willing to sit for hours and listen to erudite art talk. Time was ticking by, and she was unable to converse with the one person in the room who interested her, James.

After the meal their hostess stood to recognize "some of the noted art experts in their midst." She promised to be brief, but rambled on, enjoying the attention she had, after all, paid dearly for. After mentioning everyone there, she finally introduced the art critic James had sent to Islesboro to see Terry's paintings, a pompous man Jane had met at the gallery the night before. Now he stood ponderously and droned on, giving the details of his "discovery" that everyone in the room already knew.

Jane fixed a polite expression on her face and played restlessly with her coffee spoon, seized with a crazy urge to tap it on her coffee cup to get everyone's attention and make an announcement of her own, that Terry's cousin, James Patton, was the one who'd sent the art critic to Islesboro in the first place. No one had made mention of that fact. Obviously James hadn't wanted it known. He'd told Jane last night there wasn't anything in this for him personally.

Jane's restlessness grew as Lottie was introduced next. After expressing her heartfelt appreciation, she announced what Jane had learned that day and what, once again, everyone in the room already knew: A Terence Patton foundation was being established, its purpose to help promising young artists develop their talent. In cooperation with the foundation, Lottie's Islesboro home would be open year-round to deserving candidates screened and selected by the foundation board.

Now she can afford to be generous and let me go. . . . Jane hated herself for thinking once again the ungracious thought that had popped into her head earlier in the day as Lottie told her enthusiastically about the plans to turn the cottage into a kind of boardinghouse for "starving" artists. Lottie's intentions were undoubtedly the best, and it would do her a world of good to think that she might be giving others the same opportunity she had given her own son: to put aside practical cares about survival and develop the inner vision.

Finally, the dinner, which had turned into an ordeal for Jane, was over. By now she was in no mood to stand around and wait to see what would develop next. She made her way straight to James.

"Could we go somewhere and talk?" she asked him without any preliminaries. "Please, James, there's something I need to ask your advice on."

James felt compromised by his very presence at the dinner, which he'd come to Boston not planning to attend. All evening he'd soothed his pride by telling himself that afterward he would offer to see Jane back to her hotel, but nothing more. If the evening were prolonged in *any* way, *she* would have to make the suggestion. Now he was taken off guard by the directness of her approach, just as he had been the previous evening. A fragmented phrase popped into his mind: *the prey stalking the hunter.* Even as he dismissed it, he remembered that he had fleetingly entertained the same thought last summer at his cottage, the day he had been selecting books he wanted to keep and Jane had walked in upon him. Before she left she had been the one to suggest that they see each other later and, thus, the one responsible for beginning still another painful chapter of Patton history: James proposes to Jane again and is turned down *again.* The "prey" hadn't been seriously stalking the "hunter," it had turned out, just "teasing" him. Well, this hunter was reformed.

"Certainly," he agreed politely. "We can have a drink in the bar at your hotel. If your flight is leaving early, you'll probably want to make an early evening of it."

Jane was expecting the black Ferrari, but James was driving a Porsche now, a *white* Porsche! "You have a new car," she commented belatedly when they were driving along and then rambled on to cover her distraction. "I still have the old Lincoln. You should see the way it sticks out like a sore thumb parked outside Susan's condominium in Fort Lauderdale, where all the other tenants drive the kind of cars you drive. I was planning to sell the Lincoln and buy a little compact car. And, now, with this new thing coming up . . ."

James had a good idea those "other tenants" were men. When through a cruel joke of fate he had run into Susan McGraw, of all people, in the early fall, she had blithely assured him that Jane was making up for lost time, engaged in what Susan called the "Florida mating game."

"What 'new thing?'" he inquired when he was confident his voice wouldn't come out a surly growl.

Jane had meant to explain the offer from the McGraw company in a calm, logical fashion, but now she found herself blurting it all out, beginning with the impromptu suggestion "Helen" had offered as she was leaving the crafts co-op last summer. Shortly thereafter Susan McGraw had appeared, like a messenger of fate, and, besides providing Jane a place to go, had taken off a sample of her needlework with the promise to show it to her father. Months later the letter from Randolph McElroy had arrived, leading to yesterday's meeting with him at his office right here in Boston.

"I have no idea what to do, James! For one thing, I don't know if I really want to move back here to Boston. And how am I to know if the offer is a good one? It's all written in legal language, full of numbers, and very complicated. There's Nick Olson, who lives next door to me. He's an attorney and should know about contracts. I'd thought I'd ask him, but—"

Jane broke off as the Porsche came to a screeching halt in front of her hotel and the uniformed doorman approached to open her door. James hadn't said a single word. He looked grimly unapproachable as he thrust a bill at the doorman and escorted Jane inside.

The hotel bar was crowded and noisy. It wasn't at all the kind of atmosphere Jane would have preferred, but James didn't suggest they go somewhere quieter and she was hesitant about inviting him up to her room.

They ordered drinks and James proceeded to ask her very detailed questions about the McGraw offer. From his manner he might have been a professional business consultant, someone who had no personal stake in the discussion at all. Jane grew more and more muddled as she tried to answer his questions. Deep down she must have been expecting something more from James than just objective analysis, even after last night's revelations.

"I just can't remember the exact figures," she protested finally, pressing her fingertips to her throbbing forehead. "Why don't you look at the contract? I have it in my room."

There had been no seductive intent in her words. She hadn't even made an explicit suggestion that the two of them go up to her room. But the silence that fell between them spelled out the situation as clearly as though it had been printed in black type on white paper. They both knew what would happen if they were alone together, this time in surroundings that would permit intimacy, with no Belinda or anyone else to intervene. Jane held her breath, praying that he *would* go with her to her room . . . praying equally as hard that he *wouldn't!* When the second prayer was answered, she had to contend with her disappointment.

"Why don't you go up and get the contract?" James stood up and slipped the change on the table into his wallet, leaving a tip for the waitress. "I'll wait for you in the lobby."

Jane was given no choice but to comply. As she rode the elevator up to her floor, unlocked her door, got the contract, and rode back down to the lobby, her sense of anticlimax deepened. *Was this all that was going to happen between James and herself?* It was hard to believe that she'd come up here to Boston, prepared to settle matters with James, once and for all, only to find that in James's opinion, there was nothing to settle.

"Here's the contract."

The short tone didn't escape James's notice. He took the sheaf of papers but didn't so much as glance at them.

"I'll look it over and let you know what I think. Of course, it'll just be my opinion," he cautioned her. "You'll have to make up your own mind." He inclined his head in what evidently was a gesture of leavetaking, turned, and started walking away.

After a second of paralysis Jane followed behind him, calling *"James!"* When he stopped and turned around, she was right there, fighting the desperation that was rising inside her.

"I just wondered how long it would take you . . . and *how* are you going to let me know what you think? You don't even know my address or my telephone number."

James's expression was odd. He looked like a man caught up by strong, conflicting impulses that couldn't have anything to do with her practical reminders.

"A week at most," he said tersely and then frowned. "Your phone number's listed under your name, I assume. It's available from the information operator?"

"Why, *yes*, it's under my name," Jane replied, thinking that he meant the telephone number at the condominium might be listed under Susan's name instead.

With that assurance James seemed ready to leave once again. Suddenly Jane just couldn't bear to have him walk away without a word, a touch, a gesture. Surely there should be *something* meaningful said or done between two people who'd been through as much as she and James had been through together. It was like leaving a sentence hanging without a period or stopping a film seconds before the end.

"James," she said again, this time in a more purposeful tone. The odd expression that had been on his face moments before flashed across his features again. He said nothing, just waited.

Jane stepped up close to him and reached her arms up around his neck. "Aren't you going to kiss me good-bye?" It was part sincere request and part challenge, but the reaction was immediate, taking her breath away. The guard dropped away from James's face. Desire and savage resentment battled in the dark depths of his eyes as he looked down at her. Then he pulled her close into his arms and granted her request.

The kiss was hardly the usual version of a farewell kiss in a hotel lobby. For Jane it was what she'd been wanting since the moment she saw James the evening before, what she'd been needing and missing since the last time she was in his arms. He was the only man who could make her feel with his touch that she was merged with him in some powerful, elemental, fast-moving current. For years she'd fought the attraction, but no longer. As his mouth claimed hers roughly and his tongue razed the intimacy of her mouth, she pressed against him, mindless of a possible audience since the world at that moment consisted only of the two of them, herself and James. There was no yesterday or tomorrow, just now.

She blinked dazedly and clung to him when he broke off the kiss without easing its intensity. Then he was taking her arms from around his neck, holding her off from him while he stepped back and spoke in a harsh, breathless voice.

"There. Is that what you wanted, Jane? It doesn't change anything, you know." He dropped his hands and backed away. "I'll be in touch with you about this." He brandished the contract, turned, and was gone, leaving Jane to stand there and stare after him.

The next morning as her plane left the ground, Jane reflected on all the changes that had occurred since last June when she had headed south in the old Lincoln, feeling like a refugee. She was more confident now. First, she'd gotten her job on her own initiative and done well at it. Her ideas for promoting sales had proved to be good ones, so that her employer treated her with growing respect. Now there was the offer from the McGraw company, which, even if she decided not to take it, was ego-bolstering.

Less than six months ago Jane hadn't been sure,

deep inside, that she could support herself and get along in the world on her own. Now she knew that not only could she "get along," but she could be a "success" if she put her mind to it. And her years in seclusion on Islesboro evidently hadn't made her a social misfit. She was having no problems at all making friends in Florida.

Why, then, since her future was most promising, didn't she feel more enthusiasm? The question plagued her during the entire flight, and she came up with no truly satisfactory answers. She and Lottie had parted on the best terms. Now that Lottie had her Terence Patton Foundation to occupy her time and energy, Jane was truly free to live her own life. And James was no longer a shadowy menace in the background, waiting to assert his dominance. He hadn't even willingly admitted that the intense sexual attraction was still there between him and Jane.

Jane was free of entanglements. Her future was as boundless as the Florida sky on a clear, sunny day. Why was she breathing a small despondent sigh instead of grinning from ear to ear?

During the following week Jane began to divine an explanation of her emotional malaise that she at first vigorously rejected. The first inkling of what was wrong came when it occurred to her that she was mentally ticking off the time until James called. The first few days, whenever the telephone would ring in the evening, she would answer it, thinking, *That's not James yet. It's too soon.* When she realized she had put her life on hold, waiting for James's call, she told herself she was simply eager to make up her mind about the McGraw offer.

But it was more than that and she knew it. She

wanted to hear James's voice. She wanted to *make contact* with him. Having reached that stage of honesty with herself, Jane delved deeper. After James had called and told her his opinion, what then? If he recommended the offer as a good one, she might assume that he wanted her to come to Boston so that they would be closer, mightn't she? After all, hadn't her main reason for asking his advice really been to give him the opportunity to sway her? But what if he didn't think the McGraw offer was a good one, advised her not to come to Boston, and then said good-bye, his good deed done?

The latter possibility stirred her with such deep uneasiness that she finally understood the real nature of her suspense. Her concern wasn't whether to take the McGraw offer or turn it down, whether to move to Boston or stay here in Florida. Those decisions were important, but she could live with them, either way. The really crucial concern was *what James would recommend*, since that would be her clue as to whether he saw them as having a future together.

James called early Saturday evening. "I thought I'd catch you before you went out for the evening," he explained.

"I wasn't going out anyway." She'd have been too afraid of missing his call. "How are you, James?"

"I'm fine." His reply firmly ignored any sincere, personal element in her inquiry. "I've studied the offer the McGraw Company is making you and discussed it with several other people, whose business opinion I value." The slight pause was portentous to Jane, twisting her nerves tighter. "Frankly I don't think you should take it, Jane. It's entirely too speculative from your point of view. The guaranteed income isn't adequate compensation. That wouldn't matter, of course, if your eventual earnings from sales made up the difference, but I've checked on the McGraw Company, and the statistics don't look good to me. They need some new blood in that facet of their operation—that's for sure. It seems they've been producing the same old thing for years."

"You're right. Their kits are boring." Jane put in, her voice hollow. He didn't think she should take the offer! *He didn't want her to come to Boston.* "So you think I should turn them down."

"That's my opinion, but you'll have to weigh your own income expectations and decide for yourself. You might be far better off starting your own company and marketing your designs yourself. I'm sure I can get backers, if you're interested."

"Start my own company?" Jane echoed, sounding as overwhelmed as she felt. "James, I don't know. . . ."

"It's only a suggestion. As I've already said, you'll have to decide for yourself on all of this. I'll send the contract down to you. You can ask for other advice." He paused. "You mentioned some attorney friend, I believe."

"Nick Olson. He lives next door." Jane supplied the name and information absently, thinking fast. She could sense that James was right on the brink of terminating the conversation. He'd satisfied his obligation to her and was ready to leave the matter in her hands. Somehow she had to keep him on the phone.

"James, I wouldn't know anything at all about starting a company. Do you really think any-one would be willing to put up money and take a chance—" She broke off, the next thought striking her like a thunderbolt. Dared she suggest it? What did she have to lose? "James, why don't *you* be my backer?"

The silence went on for at least a century, even though Jane didn't think she had taken him totally by surprise. It had occurred to him that she might make the suggestion.

"I don't think I'd be the right backer for your business venture," he said finally.

"Why? Don't you have any confidence in me? Do you think my designs aren't good?" Jane pressed. He hadn't sounded *that* definite, and as long as she kept him talking, he wouldn't hang up.

"It has nothing to do with confidence or whether your designs are good." His voice was hard, accusing her of playing games with him. "I'm sure you know that. You and I can't have a purely business relationship."

Jane took the dive and plunged in. She had nothing to lose but pride, and it was a poor companion. "Why does our relationship have to be just business, James? I don't know about you, but I'd like it to be more. I made that discovery in Boston."

Another silence. "Jane, I thought I made myself clear last summer," he began, every word a battleground where temptation wrestled with pride. Jane jumped in quickly to give temptation a hand.

"James, you *did* make yourself clear!" she said fervently. "You swore you'd never ask me to marry you again. I'm not asking you to break that promise to yourself. I'm simply telling you that *I* would like a 'personal relationship' with you, whether you want to back me in a business venture, or not."

"I don't know—" He'd worked too hard nurturing

his resistance to her claim upon him to relinquish it when she snapped her fingers. "Jane, you had every chance to have the most 'personal' relationship a woman can have with a man, but you weren't interested. Why have you changed your mind?"

"James, your marriage proposal last summer was an insult. If I'd accepted, neither one of us would ever have had any respect for me. You didn't even ask me. You made a deal with Lottie to buy me, as though I were merchandise. There wasn't the first mention of love or even affection." Jane paused, steeling her courage. "If you made me the same kind of proposal now, James, I'd have to turn you down again."

"You won't have that chance," he put in grimly. "I meant what I said, Jane."

"Okay," she said gently. "I thought we'd established that. You don't have to ask me to marry you, James, not again, not *ever*. Now, are you interested in being a part of my life, or not. I'd like for you to be."

"You mean you want to have an affair?"

"Call it whatever you like," she replied calmly, refusing to take offense.

"What about the contract?" James evaded the issue, hedging for time. He was too damned proud to say yes, too damned weak to say no. "Do you want me to mail it down to you?"

Jane opened her mouth to tell him the truth—she didn't need the contract since she intended to follow his advice and turn the offer down—but then she found herself saying something entirely different.

"Why don't you bring it down to me? If you can get away, that is."

"Actually, I'm leaving tomorrow morning for a

week in St. Croix," he countered quickly and then added, as though it were just an afterthought, "I suppose I could stop off on the way back."

"Is Belinda going with you?" The little green-eyed monster just popped out. She halfway expected James to reply that it was none of her business.

"No, she isn't."

Since that question hadn't annoyed him, she risked one a little more daring whose answer was of intense interest to her. "James, is Belinda somebody . . . *special?*" His pause seemed answer enough. Suddenly she didn't want to know for sure that he was intimately involved with the lovely blonde. "That's okay. Forget I asked."

He answered anyway, in a quietly bitter voice. "No, Belinda *isn't* special, Jane. There's only one woman who was ever special in my life. That woman was you." *And still is,* he added despairingly to himself.

He hadn't entirely answered her questions. "So you aren't having an affair with Belinda?"

"No. What about you? Are you having an affair with this Nick Olson character?" He asked the question grudgingly, as though to say the answer didn't really matter to him, one way or the other.

"No, I'm not having an affair with Nick or anybody else," Jane told him earnestly. "As a matter of fact, I've never had an affair with any man besides you, James. That is, if you can call what happened with us last summer an affair."

In James's mind the term didn't fit, but he didn't say as much because he didn't want to get into a discussion of *why* it didn't fit. All he knew was that, unlike Jane, he *had* had affairs, quite a few of them, and what had happened between him and Jane hadn't *felt* like an affair to him. Making love to her had been like fulfilling his destiny, but obviously it hadn't been the same for her. The reflection brought a renewed surge of proud misgivings about getting involved with her again.

"An affair is usually a sustained sexual relationship outside of wedlock. What happened between us was more like a one-night stand," he suggested callously.

Jane was silent, remembering their lovemaking those two nights at James's cottage the past summer. " 'One-night stand,' " she repeated. "That sounds so sordid, and I didn't feel sordid at all, did you?"

"It wasn't sordid," James said brusquely, despising himself for having demeaned what had been so transcendent it defied description with mere words. "Jane, I have to go now. Are you sure . . ."

"I'm sure. You said you're going to St. Croix for a week? Then you'd be stopping here next Saturday or Sunday?" She gripped the receiver tighter, a wave of longing sweeping her as she thought of him here in this room with her. "James . . . I don't suppose you'd like to stop tomorrow, on your way down?"

"No, that wouldn't be possible." He wanted to, more than anything, but he couldn't. His pride wouldn't allow him.

Chapter Twelve

At the conclusion of the conversation James had actually agreed only to bringing Jane the contract in Fort Lauderdale on his return from St. Croix. He hadn't said he would be willing to back her in a business venture or that he was even interested in having an affair with her.

But he was coming there. Jane hung up the phone, as unaccountably lighthearted as she had been down in the dumps a week ago flying home from Boston. There was no denying that the swing in moods revolved around James. A future without James, no matter how filled with opportunities, had seemed oddly "flat." It was like a painted landscape executed with technical mastery, but without that spark that was genius.

Essentially nothing had changed. James hadn't agreed to be a part of her life, even though she knew deep down he wanted to. He was fully capable of maintaining his stubborn distance. He could come here, deliver the contract, leave, and never make contact with her again. The awareness of that possibility failed to deflate Jane's buoyant state of mind.

The next week was a busy one. New stock arrived in the shop, and she rearranged the whole needlework section. The result was most pleasing and drew very complimentary remarks from her employer.

"Looks great, Jane. You really have a knack for display. Problem is . . ." He looked ruefully around the shop. "This needlework section looks so good, it makes the rest of the place look bad by comparison! And look at the sales figures. A good third of the total business comes out of this one section. If we keep expanding it, we'll have to turn the whole place into a needlework shop."

"Not a bad idea, is it?" Jane suggested promptly with a bright smile.

Jim Garrett didn't smile in return. He eyed her seriously. "Don't think I haven't been considering that, Jane. But I couldn't take the risk unless you gave me some assurance that you intended to stick with me. You're the one personally responsible for this great surge of interest in needlework, and I know it. If you walk out the door, it won't be an easy matter replacing you."

Jane was sober, too, when she replied, aware now that the conversation wasn't an idle one. "I enjoy working here, Mr. Garrett, but right now I can't give you any promises. If you remember, the day I applied for this job I mentioned that eventually I intended to go into business on my own. Actually, right at this moment I have two different business opportunities.

Of course, I would never leave you without giving notice," she hastened to add, seeing the alarm on his face.

"What kind of business opportunities, if you don't mind my asking, Jane?" he replied readily.

Jane briefly told him about the offer from the McGraw Manufacturing Company, not mentioning that she'd almost definitely decided not to take it, and then about the suggestion from a "business adviser" that she get backers and market her own designs.

Garrett was silent a few seconds, obviously mulling over the information. "Let me know as soon as you decide. You're awfully good at what you're doing now, Jane. If you'd be interested in staying right here, we could work out something to your advantage."

Jane didn't hesitate. "If you could be more specific, Mr. Garrett, it might help me to decide."

Respect shone in his shrewd but cautious businessman's eyes. "Why don't I give it some thought, and we'll talk about it in a day or two."

"Fine," Jane agreed, and then turned her attention at once to two of her regular customers who were walking into the shop. "Hazel, I'm so glad you came in," she greeted the woman, moving toward them. "That yarn you've been waiting for came in this morning."

Jim Garrett watched her a moment to confirm what he already knew. She was in her element here in this shop, utterly confident of herself and her merchandise when she was dealing with customers interested in her own passion, needlework, which she had taken to a much higher, more artistic level than do most needlework hobbyists. He would make her a good offer and try to keep her here.

All that day Jane kept thinking of the conversation with Garrett. No matter how many times she told herself not to get her hopes raised, the feeling grew inside her that this was the opportunity that was right for her. She loved working in the shop, where her job involved so much more than just sales. She was sharing an interest and expertise. Her regular customers came to rely upon her, and she knew them all by name.

The prospect of staying on at the shop grew more and more appealing as she thought of what such a decision would mean. She would live right here in the Fort Lauderdale area, where she already had begun to make friends and to feel at home. Despite the occasional attacks of nostalgia for New England, she didn't want to move back north. She wanted to stay here in the warmth and bright sunshine where her life had blossomed. And though it was heady to think of starting her own company and being a woman executive, she would be on completely unfamiliar ground, sure of nothing except her needlework designs themselves. Sure, she could probably learn whatever would be demanded of her, but why give up what she knew she liked for the unknown?

By the time Jim Garrett called her into his office two days later, Jane was scared to death he'd either changed his mind or wouldn't make her an offer attractive enough to accept. When he offered her a limited partnership with an immediate increase in salary and a modest share of profits that would escalate over a stated period, she didn't even hesitate.

"Yes, *yes!* I'll take it," she told him eagerly.

"Don't you want to take a little time to think it over?" Garrett felt compelled to ask, although his conscience was clear. The offer was a fair one. "Isn't there someone you want to talk it over with? You mentioned a business adviser."

"No," Jane replied firmly, remembering how James had kept insisting that she would ultimately have to make up her own mind about the McGraw offer. When James came that weekend, she would be able to greet him as a completely independent woman, asking no favors, not even advice.

James had spent a restless week in St. Croix. He'd gone at the invitation of friends who owned a vacation home there and doubted they would ever bother to invite him again, since he'd been quite unsociable, spending most of his time walking on the beach alone or wandering through the streets of the nearby Frederiksted.

What he really wanted was to cut his stay short and fly to Fort Lauderdale, but he simply would not allow himself to be drawn to her like an iron shaving to a magnet. Again and again he went over the telephone conversation and her suggestion that he be her business backer, followed by the proposition, couched in euphemistic terms, that they have an affair. *You don't have to marry me,* she'd said. *I just want you to be a part of my life.*

James wasn't buying that crap. Maybe living on her own had caused her to have second thoughts about turning him down last summer. Maybe she was so used to having him dangling by a string that she just wanted to give a jerk to make sure he really hadn't cut free. Whatever her reasons, there wasn't any way in hell he could keep himself from stopping off in

Lauderdale. The need to see her again, touch her, *love* her was too powerful to subdue.

As much as Jane had been looking forward to James's arrival, when she opened the door to him on Saturday afternoon she was seized with the sense of strangeness at seeing him there in her new habitat. To cover her sudden shyness she showed him around the condominium as though he were a prospective tenant. He looked marvelous, deeply tanned from his week in the Caribbean. Jane had offered to pick him up at the airport, but he had refused. She didn't know whether he had taken a taxi or rented a car, but he wasn't carrying any luggage, just a slim leather attaché case, in which, presumably, was her contract.

"As you can see, the view from out here is marvelous," she said with forced enthusiasm, walking ahead of him to the sliding glass doors leading out on the balcony.

James set the attaché case down and followed after her, tensely aware of every muscle and nerve in his body. He hadn't expected her to be nervous and uncertain. It was disconcerting to go into battle with heavy artillery and then discover one's opponent to be unarmed.

"This is a nice place," he said, stepping out on the balcony. Jane's eyes searched his face to verify the reassurance she had heard in his voice, found it, and more, much more. The joy inside her broke free, lighting her face with a welcoming smile.

"James, I'm so glad—" she began, and got no further. He moved with that incredible swiftness that had always startled her in the past, the predator swooping down upon the prey. A most willing prey, in this instance, though it hadn't always been the case. Now as he caught her close, her arms went up around his neck, and her lips met his eagerly, trapping his whispered name in her mouth for long minutes while their lips and their tongues met in an urgent reconciliation.

"*James—*" She tried to gulp in air and get the thought out a little later, but then he was kissing her again and thought was translated into response.

They made love in Jane's bedroom. The first time was hurried and explosive, bringing the universe temporarily to an end. The second time was more leisurely, the rise of pleasure more deliberate and prolonged. Jane felt that she was an exquisite instrument skillfully and lovingly played by a master. Under the spell of James's touch she couldn't conceive of any other purpose for being except to make love with him.

"James, you are a wonderful lover," she murmured, lying contentedly beside him afterward. "I don't like to think of how you got to be so good. It makes me jealous."

James raised himself up on his elbow and looked down at her. For the pure pleasure of touching her he slid his fingers over the curve of her hips, into the dip of her waist, and then slowly upward until he could capture a rounded breast that tempted him irresistibly to taste the dark bud at the tip, sated though he was. Leaning down, he kissed the nipple and then felt a stir of pleasure and power as she relaxed even closer against him. To have her like this was worth any price. Gone was any reservation about backing her.

"Have you made up your mind yet about the McGraw offer?" he asked, nuzzling his lips against the warm satin texture of her breast.

"Yes, I've decided not to take it." Jane squeezed his head briefly against her and then gently wriggled free, sitting up. "Something a lot better has come along."

James was immediately on the alert although he tried not to show it. Lying back with his hands clasped behind his head, he asked casually, "Oh? And what's that?"

Jane told him eagerly about the limited partnership offer her present employer had made her and her own acceptance of it. Her face gradually fell with disappointment when James listened impassively and then made no response, either favorable or unfavorable.

"Well, what do you think?" she asked, impatient and slightly apprehensive. Perhaps it *wasn't* a good offer.

He shrugged. "What difference does it make what I think? It seems you've already made up your mind." Under his pretended coolness he was trying to adjust to the fact that she *didn't* want financial backing from him now. Did she want anything else? Or had he come here and let himself in for another rejection, another protracted and painful recovery?

"Do you or don't you think it sounds like a good opportunity?" she pressed, frowning down at him.

With minimal effort James raised himself up, swung his legs down to the floor, and stood up. "Judging from what you've told me, it sounds like an outstanding offer."

Something about his movements and the tone of his voice brought back dismaying memories of his behavior following each of the two times they had made love last summer in Islesboro. Was he going to make that same swift transition from passion to hostility?

"James, what are you going to do?" she asked

uneasily when he began to gather up his clothes. He answered without looking at her.

"I thought I'd take a shower, if that's all right. Unless you'd prefer I just get dressed immediately and go."

Jane jumped up from the bed. "Are—are you *going?*" she protested miserably, remembering now the absence of luggage. "Don't be silly. Of course, I don't mind if you take a shower."

James glanced around then, taking in her enormous disappointment, which she made no effort to hide.

"What do you want, Jane?" he asked tersely.

Her eyes widened with sudden hope, became clear, golden pools of questioning as she gazed back at him. "I don't want you to go, James," she said with soft pleading, taking a hesitant step toward him and then another, until the distance between them had been bridged, and they stood very close together. "That's really all I *know* right now. *I don't want you to go.*"

He nodded. It wasn't enough, not nearly enough, but better than nothing. "All right. I won't go then." He started toward the bathroom door, not trusting himself to say more.

Jane went limp with relief, and after a moment's uncertainty, followed in behind him. When James stopped at the bathroom door and turned around, she ran right into him. His arms closed around her, drawing her against him, and he had to fight hard against the sharp rise of emotion in his breast.

"I was going to ask you if you wanted to shower with me," he said gruffly.

"I thought you'd never ask," she whispered, hugging him with all her strength, rejoicing in the rapid, steady beat of his heart.

James had driven a rental car from the airport and had his luggage in the trunk. Jane carefully refrained from asking him the questions she would have liked to have had answered. Had he come to Lauderdale open to the idea of spending the weekend with her? Or had he softened toward her and been swayed by her own wishes?

For now, she dared not probe into James's thoughts and feelings. She had to seize the joy of this one weekend in his company and hope that it wouldn't be an isolated chapter in her life, but rather a beginning of a new relationship between them. Because of the past, she saw that relationship as tender and fragile, easily damaged by a wrong word or gesture.

Unbeknownst to her, Jane's caution and tentativeness worked in her favor with James. Had she been more sure of herself, he wouldn't have been able to drop his guard, put aside his suspicions, and not take, but at least longingly examine what she seemed to be offering him as a gift for the taking: Her desire for his presence and her evident pleasure in his company. It was a treasure he had tried forcibly to attain, and he just couldn't quite believe it could be free.

Yet as the weekend progressed he could ascertain nothing material that Jane wanted from him. She had her financial future well in hand. He found it incredible that she had come here to Lauderdale just six months ago, with no job experience whatever, and now was embarking on a partnership without investing a cent of capital.

"How old is this Garrett fellow?" James had inquired transparently.

"I don't know—maybe late forties," Jane had replied and then bluntly answered the question he was

really asking. "He has no interest in me as a woman, if
that's what you're thinking." She thought a moment.
"I have to admit, that would be pretty flattering,
though, to think that a man would be willing to pay
that kind of money . . ."

They were sitting together on the huge sectional
sofa in the living room. James knew she was retaliat-
ing with subtle punishment for his suspicions, but her
words raised the quite unbearable prospect of another
man possessing her. Reacting to the savage stab of
jealousy, he pushed her back on the soft pillows and
imprisoned her with the hard length of his body.

"Men have been known to pay a high price for the
women they want," he said grimly, looking down at
her face and noting the startled expression. "Sometimes they go to desperate measures—kill, kidnap—"
He broke off at her gasp. "What's wrong? Am I
hurting you?" He started to lever his body away from
her, but Jane quickly grasped his shoulders and pulled
him back down on top of her.

"You're not hurting me," she assured him softly,
and then smiled a tender, bemused smile. "For a
moment there you were acting out this fantasy that I
have about you."

James was immediately intrigued and insisted that
she describe it to him. Jane complied, slightly embarrassed. "You're my sexy 'knight,' James, in a black
bathing suit," she concluded sheepishly. "You've always worn black bathing suits, haven't you?"

"I suppose I have," James answered, pulling free of
her and sitting up on the edge of the sofa. Any man
would be flattered to be a woman's recurring erotic
fantasy, but James found himself deeply disturbed by
Jane's revelation. Was sex what she wanted from him?

"You mind, don't you?" Jane was asking in a small, apologetic voice.

"No," James lied. As he slipped his hands under her short knit top and slowly pushed it up, baring her breasts to his sight, he was hearing in his mind her soft, satisfied woman's voice, *You're a wonderful lover, James.* Bending forward, he pressed his lips to her midriff and then slowly gazed upward, feeling her indrawn breath and hearing the question in his whispered name. She wasn't convinced that he didn't mind. Not heeding the question, he took his time about reaching a breast, giving it time to grow heavy with waiting. The nipple was stiff against his tongue when he took it into his mouth. This time when she said *James!* it wasn't a question, but an affirmation of her passion and a plea that he proceeded to grant. If sexual pleasure was what she wanted from him, he would give it to her, in full measure, and try not to think of the time when she might grow tired of him, replace him with another fantasy.

Sunday night, snuggled next to James in bed, Jane thought of being in it alone the next night and sighed. "I guess you have to go tomorrow, don't you?" So far there had been no mention between them of his coming to see her again.

James let her interpret his silence as acquiescence. He was a busy man, with many demands upon his time, but someone of his wealth didn't ever *have* to do anything or be anywhere. A few telephone calls and he could stay right here. But he didn't think that was in his best interest.

"Will you come again?" she asked softly.

"If I'm invited, I will."

Jane hugged him happily. "You're invited next

weekend and the next and the next. Just consider it an open invitation."

James came the following weekend, and once again they didn't leave the condominium. They talked, laughed, prepared simple meals, and made love. Once or twice it was on the tip of Jane's tongue to tease James about having an insatiable sexual appetite, but she held back the words, still not sure enough of their relationship.

"Can you come again next weekend?" she asked hopefully on Sunday evening and then fell asleep, happy, when he agreed.

When he arrived the following Friday evening, Jane was building up her nerve to tell him about the plans she had made. "I thought we could go car-shopping tomorrow. I've just *got* to get another car soon. And then Sunday afternoon—" She had to muster her courage and keep going when she saw the expression on James's face, which she took to be objection. "I hope you don't mind, James, but I've invited a few people over, Jim Garrett and his wife, Pam, Nick Olson next door and his girlfriend, Elise. I want them to meet you." The odd look on James's face *wasn't* objection. She didn't know what it was.

"Mind? Why should I mind?" he said quietly, and took her into his arms and held her very tightly in an embrace that wasn't sexual.

Jane hugged him hard around the waist. "James, I missed you. I've got so much to *tell* you," she said happily. "It's been a hectic week. I'm afraid I haven't even managed to get to the supermarket. We'll have to go out and get something to eat."

"Sure." His arms loosened and he leaned back to see her face. "You want to go now—or later."

She thought she understood what he was asking her: Did she want to eat before or after they made love. Her answer was a trifle apologetic. "Do you mind if we go now? I skipped lunch today, and I'm starving."

James raised his eyebrows. "That's what happens when a person changes from an employee to his or her own boss. Out the window go coffee breaks, lunch hours. Just watch out for the weekends," he threatened lightly.

Jane relaxed then, knowing intuitively that her hopes for this weekend were going to work out. She wanted James to be a part of her *whole* life, not just her weekend lover. He seemed willing.

"Can you believe it'll be Christmas in a few weeks?" she asked him later that evening. They had returned to the condominium and were having a glass of wine out on the balcony, with the restless sounds of the Atlantic in the foreground. "It just doesn't *seem* like Christmas without snow and ice."

James shrugged and made a noncommittal answer to the effect that Christmas wasn't a big traditional holiday for him as it was for most people. He usually spent it in some sunny holiday spot.

"What are your plans for Christmas this year?" Jane persisted, somewhat irked that he wasn't being more cooperative and taking the conversation in the direction she'd intended it to go.

"What are *your* plans?" he countered. "Are you going up to Jacksonville to be with your mother?"

"No, I'll just be taking off Christmas day from the shop. Business has already picked up with the gift buying. I'm offering a free workshop with the purchase of a needlework kit for a gift. My classes are jammed right now, with everyone madly working to complete projects for gifts."

"You'll be staying here, then."

She nodded encouragingly, waited, and then lost patience. "You still haven't answered my question. Where will you be at Christmas?"

"Assuming that I'm invited, I'll be here with you."

"Of *course,* you're invited!" she replied in exasperation. "What do you think this whole conversation is about?" Her voice changed to pleading. "From now on, until further notice, would you please 'assume' that you're always 'invited?' "

James **nodded briefly**. "Until further notice."

Jane let **the remark** go by, but the whole exchange warned her that she would not be able to rush James. He still was holding back, maintaining his proud distance. She was going to have to be patient, very patient, until he learned to trust her.

"What would you like for a Christmas present?" he asked casually, cutting into her sober thoughts.

Jane got up from her chair and walked around behind his. "Nothing except you," she said softly, running her hands along his shoulders and then bending forward to kiss the top of his head.

James grasped one of her hands and drew her around his chair so that he could pull her down on his lap. She came willingly and settled into his arms. "Come on. Surely you must want something. Why don't you let me buy you a new car? Something fast and sporty that I can drive when I'm here on weekends."

"No." Jane wound her arms a little tighter around his neck and kissed him on the lips to emphasize her refusal. "You don't need to buy me a car. I can buy my own car."

"It's too hot here for furs. What about a piece of jewelry? Tell me what you like. Diamonds, sapphires, rubies—"

"No, no, *no!*" Jane punctuated each *no* with a kiss and then teased the outline of his mouth with the tip of her tongue. Her breath was coming faster as she breathed in the clean masculine smell of him, responded to his closeness. "Keep your money, James," she murmured. "Just come and be with me, like this . . . . Now, could we please make love? Hmmm?"

For all his mental reservations, it was a request James couldn't hope to deny after a week apart from her.

The months passed and James continued to come each weekend, arriving on Friday evening and leaving Monday morning, until finally one Monday morning, in an unguarded moment, Jane finally voiced what had been building up inside her, the wish for something more than their weekend relationship.

When her alarm clock went off, she sat up sleepily in bed, blurting out the first thought that came to her mind. "Oh, *damn*. I *wish* you didn't have to *leave*. I wish you *lived* here. James, why don't you move to Fort Lauderdale? I don't guess that's possible, is it?" She sat with her knees drawn up, her elbows braced on them, and her shoulders slumped over, dejected at her own realistic conclusion.

James had been awake before the alarm clock buzzed. He had been lying there, thinking of a week without her, before he could come back. Lately the situation had grown more intolerable for him, but he'd been putting off this conversation that suddenly seemed imminent.

"Anything's possible," he replied carelessly.

Jane stared down at him, not quite believing her ears. "Do you mean it?" she demanded excitedly. "Could you really move here to Lauderdale?"

He shrugged. "Sure." Aware of her intense scrutiny, James carefully schooled his features to look casual because he didn't feel in the least casual about what he was about to suggest. "If I get a place here, will you live with me?"

Jane looked away from him, deeply disappointed, not just by the offhanded proposal, but by his manner, which she knew was a coverup for his feelings. He cared about her answer, and yet he wasn't willing to let her see that he cared. After all this time, he still didn't trust her. He still couldn't swallow his pride. Well, she had been patient with him and his pride long enough.

"No, James, I will not *live* with you!" Jane hurled the refusal over her shoulder, threw back the sheet and got out of bed, where she stood, glaring at him. When he lay there perfectly still, not uttering a word of rebuttal or showing any emotion whatever, she picked up her dressing gown and managed to put it on, her hands shaking so hard that she had trouble tying the satin robe around her waist. With all her heart now she was wishing that she had gotten up as usual today and stumbled about getting dressed, but it was too late now. What had been begun had to be finished.

"Well? Don't you have anything to *say* about that?"

she demanded belligerently, wanting him to argue with her.

"What is there to say, Jane?" came his terse reply. "I can't force you to live with me if you don't wish to."

"What is there to say!" Jane repeated incredulously and then again in a tone of growing outrage. "What is there to *say!* I'll tell you what there is to say, James Patton! You can say you're acting like a proud, arrogant fool, and what you really want is not for me to live with you, but to marry you! That's what you can *say*—" Jane swallowed hard as her voice cracked on the last word. She hugged her arms tight across her chest and blinked, trying desperately not to break down crying, at least until she had finished telling him all she wanted to say.

James sat up slowly. "Why should I say that, Jane?" he asked with a deadly calm that didn't reveal the tumult inside him. When she just stared at him, helplessly shaking her head, he continued in the same tone. "Why should I think you would want to marry me now, when you never wanted to marry me before?"

"James, I never *loved* you before," Jane pointed out despairingly. "You never loved *me* before. And you do now—or at least I thought you did." She searched his face imploringly. "Don't you?"

The harsh denial in his face made her turn away. She buried her face in her hands, swept by a sense of disbelief and hopelessness. She had been so *sure* he loved her, too, and was just reticent about expressing emotion in words.

"You're wrong about one thing, Jane." He spoke

from just behind her, the words sounding as though they'd been dredged up from inside him. "You may not have loved me before, but I always loved you." His hands closed hard over her shoulders.

Jane whirled around, joy breaking out over her face. She knew those were the hardest words James had ever had to speak in his life, and she treasured them all the more for their enormous cost in lost pride.

"I love you *now*, James, with all my heart!" she told him softly.

The fierce light of love and possession burned brighter in his dark eyes, but the pride was still there, lingering in the depths, preventing him from asking her what he needed to know. Jane smiled at him, her eyes lucid and golden with understanding.

"I love you the way I've never loved any man, James. You're my 'knight,' and you always will be." And because his emotion was too intense, too painful for him, she added huskily, "My sexy knight in a black bathing suit!"

Crushed against the hard, supple body that she had admired long before she loved him, Jane was soon well aware that her knight wasn't wearing a black bathing suit at the moment. He wasn't wearing anything at all. Close upon that realization came another. James wouldn't catch his nine o'clock flight that morning. And Jane wouldn't get to work on time. . . .